KLAND

Bay

E

E

The Great Wall of Wonrek

River Ramat

Rock
Splatt
Padstow
Washaway
van Blystra
The
Crystal
Pool
Nimdob

Nimdob Gaol

E

E

Eden Valley

Polperro

The
Polperro
Inn

ungle
Dome

Desert
Dome

Dolphineers

Jack Truro
with the
Amulet of Hope
and the
Bright Beam
of the
White Wand

Melanchol Drym
and Dribble

Warleggan, Wendron,
and Scratchit

Kernowland

Colosseum of Dread

Book Six

Titles available in the Kernowland series:

To our darling granddaughter,
Olivia.

Merry Christmas
All our love,
Nanny & Bamps

Kernowland

Colosseum of Dread

Jack Trelawny

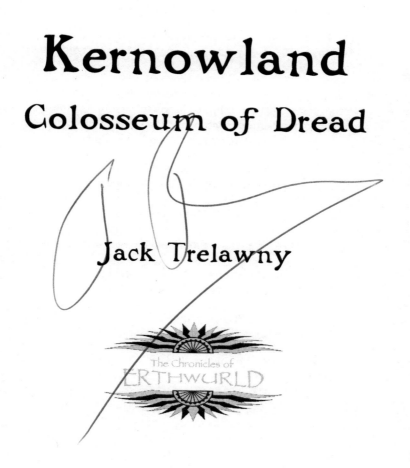

The Chronicles of
ERTHWURLD

CAMPION BOOKS

A catalogue record for this book
is available from the British Library

ISBN 978-1-906815-00-4

Campion Books is an Imprint of Campion Publishing Limited

Illustrations by Marlene Keeble
and Louise Hackman-Hexter

Printed in the UK by
CPI Group (UK) Ltd, Croydon, CR0 4YY

First published in the UK in 2009 by

CAMPION BOOKS
2 Lea Valley House
Stoney Bridge Drive
Waltham Abbey
Essex, UK
EN9 3LY

www.kernowland.com
www.erthwurld.com

For Tizzie and Louis

Illustrations:
The front cover illustration was produced by Marlene Keeble.
The illustrations of Tizzie and Louis, and the back endpaper,
were produced by Louise Hackman-Hexter.
The front endpaper contains elements from both illustrators.

AUTHOR'S  NOTES

Apart from Tizzie & Louis,
the characters and events in this book
are entirely fictitious.

In the *Erthwurld* books,
'Erth' means 'Earth',
and 'Wurld' means 'World'.
Evile is pronounced *ee-vile* to rhyme with mile.
Skotos is pronounced *skoh-toss* – it means 'darkness' in Greek.
Photos is pronounced *foh-toss* – it means 'of light' in Greek.
Graph means 'draw' in Greek, so a *photograph* is…
'a picture drawn with light'.

Websites
There is lots of other information
as well as clickable zooming maps
on the Kernowland and Erthwurld websites

www.kernowland.com
www.erthwurld.com

ONE

An Ominous Rumbling

'Urghh… w… water.'

Little Louis groaned.

His mouth was dry from extreme thirst.

He was hanging by his ankles from a post.

They were red raw from the rubbing of the rope.

His shirt and trousers were torn.

His arms dropped down towards the ground.

He'd been upsified the previous evening.

And had been hanging there, suspended upside down, throughout a long, cold, dark night.

It was now morning. The sun was rising in the east.

'Urghh…'

Louis groaned again.

He was hungry from lack of food.

And groggy from lack of sleep.

All the blood had run to his head.

It was then that he heard it.

Rrmmblrrmmblrrmmblrrmmbl…

An ominous rumbling, grumbling, sound in the distance.

Like thunder on the ground.

It was getting louder and louder by the second.

That could only mean one thing.

Whatever was making the sound…

…was heading his way.

TWO

The Gathering Storm

Lone Eagle spoke from the Crystal Well.

Again, it was as if Tizzie could hear his voice in her ears *and* inside her head at the same time.

'The Council of Guardians of The One Light has sent me here from the Rainbow Realm to talk to you, the good people of Erthwurld, to ask for your help.

'We, the Light Guardians of the Rainbow Realm, are constantly working in the cause of Good and Right on our side of life, fighting the Dark Lord, Devillian, and his Demons of Darkwurld, a terrible place where the only light is fire.

'This conflict has waged in all the many dimensions of existence throughout eternity.

'But The Darkness has been gathering like a storm cloud over your wurld, as more and more of your people choose the Dark Path and turn away from The Light.

'The time is coming in Erthwurld for a Great Battle between Good and Evil... Right and Wrong...

'...Darkness and Light.'

THREE

Dog On A Post

RRMMBLRRMMBLRRMMBLRRMMBL...

As the morning light allowed him to see more of his surroundings, Louis turned his head a little to the left, towards the source of the rumbling thunder.

Everything looked so different upside down.

All he could see was a bridge over a big river.

The sound was coming from beyond the bridge; from down the road, behind the hills on the horizon.

Trying to take everything in, he turned his head to the right.

His eyes met a very strange sight.

About twenty paces away, also upsified on a post, and hanging by his hind legs, was a little brown sausage dog.

The dog had unusually long ears.

They were drooping down towards the ground.

Louis loved dogs.

He smiled and tried to be friendly.

'Hello, doggy.'

The dog looked away, as if he was actually ignoring Louis.

Now Louis heard a voice inside his head.

He knew it was the dog's thoughts he was hearing.

'*That's the boy who killed the King and Queen.*'

Louis found himself replying out loud.

'I didn't kill the King and Queen. I'm innocent!'

RRMMBLRRMMBLRRMMBLRRMMBL...

FOUR

The Ultimate Weapon Of Death

Tizzie leant forward in her seat as Lone Eagle continued.

'The outcome of the Great Battle will decide whether Darkness or Light will rule in your wurld for the next thousand years.

'With the elixir that keeps him alive, Evile has been able to take power in Erthwurld and expand his Dark Empire for centuries.

'This has enabled him to carry out the bidding of his master, Devillian, the Lord of Darkness.

'It is a great misfortune that Devillian has now been able to lead his Forces of Darkness in your wurld to find *Skotos*, his ultimate weapon of death sent into Erthwurld from Darkwurld.

'And, worse still, the magician, Violothan, has chosen to follow the Dark Path.

'Violothan is a powerful sorcerer, and has the ability to wield the Death Stone to produce the Dark Beam in Erthwurld.

'The power of *Skotos* and its Dark Beam has already been shown in the destruction of Kernowland's major defence system, the Forcesphere.

'So it is now imperative that the Followers of The Light join together and rise up against the Dark Lord and his Forces of Darkness.'

Lone Eagle paused as Hiawatha stood to speak.

'All present have heard the terrible news about the fall of Kernowland, Lone Eagle. And we are all willing to give our lives

10

in the cause of Good and Right. But how are we to fight such a weapon as *Skotos*?'

'Murmamurmamurma... Murmamurmamurma...'

This caused a murmuring around the assembly of rebels before Lone Eagle spoke again.

'Another Light Guardian will now address you.'

With that, Lone Eagle's image began to fade.

Almost immediately, another three-dimensional image made of light began to form in its place.

Tizzie heard gasps of amazement around the Powwow Tipi as people recognised the new visitor.

'*Godolphin the Great!...*'

FIVE

A Fine Story

RRMMBLRRMMBLRRMMBLRRMMBL...

As the approaching rumble got louder and louder, Louis heard someone speak.

'Well, they all say that, don't they?'

The young boy looked across the road at another upsified person.

He was very short, and very fat, with white hair and a white beard. He also had very red cheeks, made even rosier than normal due to hanging upside down for such a long time.

He was wearing blue dungarees, with a name stitched on the front... **PLUMPER**

'They all say what?' said Louis.

The fat person spoke again.

'All prisoners say they're innocent.'

'But I DIDN'T kill the King and Queen!'

'Well, who did then?'

'It was the King's nephew, Manaccan,' said Louis. 'He killed his uncle and his aunt with that tall wizard's help... the one with the violet robes... and Dr Lizard was on their side too.'

'A fine story,' said the little person.

'But it's *true*,' said Louis, as a little tear formed in his eye in frustration at the injustice of it all. 'Mr Sand saved my life by jumping in front of me. Princess Kea stabbed her cousin, Prince Manaccan, because he killed her mum and dad. I used my catapult and there was a huge explosion and everything went crazy and Mr Sand told me to run away. That's what really happened.'

'Hmmm,' said Plumper, as if he may just be willing to give Louis the benefit of the doubt. 'I must admit, all of us gnomes knew it was a pack of lies what was on those *Wanted* posters; when they said that Clevercloggs, Princess Kea, and Mr Sand had all been responsible for the destruction of the Forcesphere and the death of the King and Queen and were now on the run because of it. We all blamed you.'

'Thanks!' said Louis.

'But now it would seem that you, Prince Louis, the so-called *Assassin Boy*, may have been innocent too.'

Louis suddenly didn't care what Plumper thought about him any more.

He had just realised the importance of the last but one thing the fat little gnome had said.

'So... Mr Sand is... is... *alive*?'

RRMMBLRRMMBLRRMMBLRRMMBL...

SIX

Godolphin The Great

'Wow!'

Now Tizzie heard Jack gasp as they both stared in awe at the brightly glowing image of Godolphin the Great.

The famous magician had long since passed over to the Rainbow Realm, but he still had the same magnetic presence that drew the gaze of all people. They just had to look at him.

The whole tent seemed to be filled with a vibrant light and buzzing energy as Godolphin now spoke.

'When living on the Erth, I used *Photos* in the cause of Good and Right, to enhance Life for as many people as possible.

'But it was my constant fear that *Skotos* would be found and come into the possession of a dark magician who could use the Death Stone to produce the Dark Beam.

'I feared that the White Light Beam from my White Wand may not have been strong enough to defeat it.

'Then I had the Dream of the *Amulet*. The Guardians of The One Light showed me the location of Seven Rainbow Crystals, which, when brought together, would boost the power of *Photos* should it ever be needed to do battle with *Skotos*. I found the Seven Rainbow Crystals and forged the magical copper *Amulet* containing them. Then, as I was shown in the dream, I set *Photos* in the middle of the *Amulet* and it began to glow, as if it had come alive.

'When wearing the *Amulet* around my neck, my whole being glowed with The One Light. I found I could then use my White

Wand to produce the Bright Beam, the brightest light on Erth, which was an even more powerful force for Healing and Good.

'But when I was nearing the end of my time on Erth, I began to fear something else. My concern was that, once I was gone, the *Amulet* would be taken and destroyed by the Forces of Darkness, leaving the way clear for *Skotos* and the Dark Beam to dominate the wurld.

'So I removed the Eight Crystals from the *Amulet* and scattered them far and wide in hiding places all over Erthwurld.

'It was my greatest hope that one day there would be another Rainbow Wizard who could find the Eight Crystals, and wield my White Wand whilst wearing the *Amulet* to produce the Bright Beam.

'There is now only one such surviving wizard who could do this. He is the last of the good Rainbow Wizards.

'Although still only an apprentice, I believe he may have enough of the *Three Qualities* – Knowledge, Wisdom, Love – to find the Eight Crystals and produce the Bright Beam with the *Amulet* and my White Wand.

'That apprentice is here today... in this very tipi.'

With that, Godolphin the Great stretched out his hand and a ball of white light formed in his palm.

Along with everyone else in the tent, Tizzie watched as the ball floated up through the air in her direction, finally coming to rest some way above her head. The ball then shot out a beam of light. The beam bathed the teenage boy sitting beside her in a bright pool of light, a bit like a spotlight on a stage.

All eyes were now on Jack.

SEVEN

The Emperor's Entourage

RRMMBLRRMMBLRRMMBLRRMMBL...

'Oh, yes, Mr Sand is very much alive,' said Plumper. 'As I said, he's on the run with Clevercloggs and Princess Kea.

'Wanted posters of the four of you have been put up all over the Kingdom. All over Erthwurld, actually, we heard.'

Even though he was wanted for a murder he didn't commit, and hanging upside down on a post facing almost certain death in the Conquest Colosseum – and he had no idea where his big sister was, or even if she was still alive – Louis felt a moment of pure joy at the thought that his friend, Mr Sand, had survived the chaos and destruction in the Prism Chamber.

Encouraged greatly by this fantastic news, Louis asked something that he'd been wondering about all night: 'Why are we hanging here like this?'

'The Emperor's coming to inspect his new territory. He enjoys seeing everyone he doesn't like upsified along the road before we fight in the Colosseum. For some reason he hates gnomes... And he hates dogs...

'And he must hate you as well.'

'Why do you say that?' asked Louis.

'Because you've been hung first in line with the gnome and the dog.'

RRMMBLRRMMBLRRMMBLRRMMBL...

EIGHT

Jack's Test

Jack squirmed in his seat, not relishing being in the glare of the spotlight and the gaze of all those present as Godolphin spoke directly to him.

'As you know, the Seven Rainbow Crystals and *Photos*, the *Crystal of Light*, are spread throughout Erthwurld.

'I hid one gem stone on each of the eight continents. You have already found the Red Crystal, here in Acirema North.

'I cannot tell you where the others are, young man.

'The test of your worthiness to wield the *Amulet* and produce the Bright Beam from the White Wand will be whether you can find and retrieve *all* of the Eight Crystals.

'My map will help you if you can use it well.

'I know you have friends to help.

'They are some of the best friends you could hope for.

'May The One Light be with you all.'

Godolphin then vanished and the mat floated down to cover the Crystal Well once more.

Hiawatha moved on to the mat so that he was standing in the centre of the tipi.

The wise old warrior then addressed everyone present by turning slowly as he spoke.

'The Guardians of The One Light have made it clear that a Great Battle between Darkness and Light is soon to be upon us.

'It is time for the rebellion against Evile to begin.

'We have each been called upon to choose whether we are going to follow the Dark Path or the Path of Light.

'If we choose Light, it is our duty to stand up and be counted, and fight for the cause of Good and Right.

'All those who choose The Light should stay.

'Those not able to commit should leave.'

Everyone stayed in their seats.

'That is pleasing,' said Hiawatha.

'I now call upon Clevercloggs the Explorer to speak.'

NINE

Marching Men

RRMMBLRRMMBLRRMMBLRRMMBL...

The source of the ground thunder now came into view as the Emperor's entourage approached the newly-named, 'Ramat Bridge', into Wonrekland.

Although it was difficult to see whilst he was hanging upside-down, Louis tried his best to take everything in.

MRCHMRCHMRCHMRCHMRCHMRCHMRCH...

The Imperial Guard Infantry came first. The big bridge shook under the strain as the foot soldiers marched over it in their sandalboots. The marching men all looked straight ahead as they filed past. Each wore a metal helmet and a short, wide sword. Some carried muskets over their shoulders.

A soldier in the middle of the front rank carried a long pole with a huge golden 'E' shape on the top of it. He was the Emperor's standard bearer.

All the marching soldiers wore Evstika armbands. Large red Evstika flags were carried at intervals of one hundred men by a centurion wearing a different type of helmet with a red plume.

Behind the infantry came a huge rectangular carriage, rolling along on sixteen wheels, with purple curtains draping down on all sides. It was drawn by sixteen enormous, mutant, purple horses. Evstika flags fluttered from each of its corners.

The carriage stopped opposite Louis. He saw a long, thin, gnarled finger point at him through the purple curtains.

TEN

'We Plan To Strike'

Clevercloggs rose from his seat to speak: 'Now that you have all agreed to take part, the RAE Rebellion is underway. But, if we are to succeed, we need the support of all the good people of Erthwurld. We can only win if we *All* work together as *One* against the tyrant... "Onen hag Oll", as we say in Kernowland. We plan to strike whilst Evile and all his cronies are in one place; at the Gladiator Games in the new Conquest Colosseum. Those gruesome games are imminent. There's no time to lose. We have much to do before they begin. A small group of us will go with the young wizard on a quest to find and collect the remaining Crystals of the *Amulet*.'

'Do you already have the *Amulet* itself... and Godolphin's White Wand?' asked Brendon Blarney. His daughter, Emily, had persuaded him to come to the Powwow at the last minute, rather than go back to Kroy Wen City, so they had flown in with Cule.

'No, but we have made plans to recover them both,' said Clevercloggs. 'We *Questers* will now travel to the other seven continents to retrieve the remaining crystals of the *Amulet* and, at the same time, talk to the good leaders and tell them of the plan for the uprising. Hopefully we can convince the good people of all the continents to join a wurldwide RAE Force in rebellion against the Empire.'

Everyone cheered when Clevercloggs had finished speaking as they thought it was a great plan.

ELEVEN

Evil Incarnate

'Soo. That'ss thee troublesomee boyy?'

The voice behind the curtains was hissing and horrible; as if its owner was as nasty as anyone could possibly be. It reminded Louis of something Mr Sand had said about the Emperor...

'Evil incarnate'.

Louis knew what that meant: 'Evil living in a human body'.

He now heard another person speaking inside the carriage.

He recognised the voice immediately.

It was Manaccan the Merciless.

'Yes, Your Imperiousness. The boy tried to thwart our plans in the Prism Chamber. He saw what happened to the King and Queen but we blamed him for it. So it's a good job we'll soon be rid of him. It seems he'd been working with my cousin, and Sand, and Clevercloggs all along.'

Your Imperiousness, thought Louis. That can only mean one thing... it *is* Evile the Emperor.

'Ii hatee thatt interferingg gnomee,' said the Emperor.

'The boy has been upsified for your pleasure on the road into Wonrekland,' snivelled Manaccan. 'Along with all the other criminals who will be fighting in the Conquest Colosseum at Enrobmac.'

The evil voice spoke again.

'Goodd, Manaccann, goodd...

'Ii amm muchh pleasedd.'

TWELVE

The *RAE Force Of Acirema North*

Once the cheering for Clevercloggs had subsided, he chaired the gathering in the Powwow Tipi as more detailed plans for the rebellion were made.

The Redskin chiefs, the leaders of the Settlers, and the Guardians of Kernow all contributed as the rebels debated who would do what and when.

The gathering came to an end once the plans had been made and Clevercloggs summarised the agreement.

'From this moment on, the Redskins and Settlers will form a joint group to be known as the *RAE Force of Acirema North*.

'This force will operate under the joint command of Princess Pocahontas and General Blarney, and will join with Admiral Crumplehorn's Guardians of Kernow to carry out the plan we have decided upon.'

Everyone nodded their agreement.

The *Questers* said their goodbyes to all their friends and gathered outside the tipi.

Tizzie looked around the little group to which she now felt she belonged and that had such important work to do: Clevercloggs, Gwithian Sand, Princess Kea, Jack Truro, and, of course, Misty, the little blue mouse, who was poking his head out of Cleverclogg's pocket. Her friends were all kind, and good, and true... but she found herself wondering how they could possibly triumph against the might of an Evil Empire.

'We'd better get moving if we're going to find the Crystals of the *Amulet* and convince the leaders of the continents to join in the RAE Rebellion,' said Clevercloggs.

With that, they walked quickly to the outskirts of Tipi City.

Since they were in Acirema North, Tizzie guessed that they'd be using the Golden Key to go back to the Golden Cavern; and then they could use the Crystal Door to travel quickly around Erthwurld.

Once she and her friends had all lined up with their hands on each other's shoulders as before, Clevercloggs bent down and touched the crystal end of the Golden Key on the ground.

He then uttered the words, '*Golden Cavern, by the power of Godolphin*'.

The line of *Questers* disappeared into the grass.

THIRTEEN

Insomnia The Ice Maiden

RRMMBLRRMMBLRRMMBLRRMMBL...

As the Emperor's carriage moved on, Louis saw it had a platform at the back.

Standing on the platform, with her head above the carriage so she had a good all-round view, was a *very* tall, very muscular woman, whose skin was pale blue.

Her bikini was the same colour as her skin.

She was completely surrounded by a fine, freezing mist that seemed to ooze from her every pore.

She had long blonde hair made wet and straggly from the moisture of the mist.

An array of weapons surrounded her, some supported on bars, others on hooks.

Louis was certain he knew who she was, from Mr Sand's description when he was learning all about Erthwurld.

She was a mutant, bred specially for her purpose.

She was as fast as a cheetah.

As strong as ten men.

An expert in all martial arts.

And she never, *ever*, slept.

She was the Emperor's personal bodyguard.

She was infamous throughout Erthwurld.

She was... *Insomnia the Ice Maiden*.

FOURTEEN

The South Pole!

As soon as the *Questers* had arrived back in the Golden Cavern, Mr Sand spoke with a sense of urgency in his voice.

'We must find the location of the next Rainbow Crystal without delay.'

'Yes, we haven't got much time,' agreed Clevercloggs.

'As we speak, Evile and all his cronies will be arriving here in our homeland to gloat over their newly-conquered territory.

'And the Gladiator Games will start very soon.

'That means lots of innocent people will be killed in the Conquest Colosseum.

'We must do all we can to prevent the slaughter.'

Everyone readily agreed.

They looked at the Godolphin Map for their next destination.

Jack pointed his wand.

'*Golow an mappa.*'

An orange light began blinking on the map.

Tizzie had exclaimed aloud before she could stop herself.

'The South Pole!'

FIFTEEN

Carriages Full Of Cronies

RRMMBLRRMMBLRRMMBLRRMMBL...

Louis watched, trying to take in as much as he could from his upside-down perspective.

Following on behind the Emperor's carriage were dozens of smaller carriages.

Louis didn't know it but they each contained a selection of Evile's cronies.

There were kings, chiefs, and all manner of other representatives of all the lands and territories of Erthwurld.

Everyone was aware that the conquering of Kernowland, the little Kingdom of Light that had held out for so long against the Empire of Darkness, was very important to the Evile.

And everyone knew how much the Emperor liked Gladiator Games.

All these kings and chiefs, and other cronies, therefore knew how important it was to make the effort to travel and be seen at the first games of the Conquest Colosseum.

'Jrrrrrrr!'

'Hsssss!'

The cronies all pointed and jeered and hissed at Louis as the carriages rumbled on past him.

RRMMBLRRMMBLRRMMBLRRMMBL...

SIXTEEN

Blizzardland

'Hmm, the South Pole in Blizzardland,' mused Mr Sand. 'That means we'll need some warm clothes.'

'Yes, indeed we will,' agreed Clevercloggs, with a knowing nod. 'I lost part of my little finger to frostbite last time I was there over a hundred years ago. As he spoke, he held up his hand so that everyone could see his stubby pinkie with its missing tip and fingernail. 'Even after all this time, it still aches sometimes.'

Tizzie couldn't decide whether it was a good or a bad thing to be as old as Clevercloggs and to have had so many exciting but dangerous adventures during the centuries that he'd been exploring Erthwurld.

'Ever since that time, I've made sure I've got the right clothes in my special rucksack for any journey to anywhere in Erthwurld,' continued Clevercloggs.

With that, he picked up his rucksack, and said, 'South Pole, Blizzardland, Acitcratna,' out loud as he opened the cords at the top.

Now he put his hand in and withdrew some thick, warm gloves, a warm coat, and boots that looked ideal for a cold climate. That rucksack is *definitely* not big enough for everything that's in it, thought Tizzie.

'Well, that's Clevercloggs sorted,' said Mr Sand, 'but, for this journey, the rest of us will need the *Traveller's Tunnel*.'

SEVENTEEN

Carry Carts And Rotten Tomatoes

RRMMBLRRMMBLRRMMBLRRMMBL...

Following on behind the crony carriages were lots and lots and lots of carry carts. Wherever he went, the Emperor and his entourage needed a very large amount of food, drink, and other provisions. As well as a whole army of servants. The carts full of servants and provisions rolled on and on.

Louis watched them rumble past.

RRMMBLRRMMBLRRMMBLRRMMBL...

Tmttt! Suddenly, a rotten tomato hit Louis on the nose.

Cbgg! Then a bit of smelly cabbage hit him on the forehead.

Tmtt! Cbgg! Tmtt!

Now Plumper and Dribble were getting the same treatment.

Lots of the servants were standing up in their carts chucking things at them. They were sneering and jeering.

'Have some of that!' Tmtt!

'And this!' Cbgg!

It was as if it were a game they had enjoyed before: pelting the upsified criminals with rotten vegetables and fruit.

Louis closed his eyes and screwed up his face. He hoped and hoped the pelting would stop soon. Some of the vegetables weren't at all soft... and he was getting bruises all over.

RRMMBLRRMMBLRRMMBLRRMMBL...

Finally the pelting ceased as the carts moved on.

Louis opened his eyes once more.

EIGHTEEN

The Traveller's Tunnel

The *Questers* walked over to two door-sized holes on one side of the Golden Cavern. There was a sign in the middle above them: *Traveller's Tunnel*.

The door holes were completely black. Tizzie couldn't see anything beyond their thresholds. The left hole had *Entrance* above it and the right hole had *Exit* above it.

'The tunnel was made by Godolphin,' explained Clevercloggs, 'because he knew that people using the Crystal Door would need different clothes and other things for some of the destinations they would be travelling to. All you need to do is think about your destination when you walk in the entrance... and you'll exit with everything you need for the journey.'

'I'll go first,' said Mr Sand. 'And I'd better take this little fellow in with me.' Tizzie could see he was holding Misty in his open palm.

Mr Sand walked in the *Entrance* hole and instantly emerged from the *Exit*. To Tizzie's amazement, he was now completely kitted out in clothes for a cold place: coat, gloves, balaclava, and boots. The clothes were all white.

Misty had a warm coat on too, which covered everything except his paws. Luckily, he also had four little boots to keep his paws warm.

Now it was Tizzie's turn. When she entered she made sure to think of the South Pole. She felt a sort of tickling all over her body, before emerging from the *Exit* with warm white clothes and boots on, just like Mr Sand had done.

When everyone had been through the Traveller's Tunnel, Clevercloggs spoke in a very serious tone.

'Acitcratna is the coldest, driest, highest, and windiest continent in Erthwurld.

'That's why they call it *Blizzardland*.

'Just a few seconds exposure to the cold and wind can result in the sort of severe frostbite that took my fingertip.

'Make sure you keep your skin covered at all times until I, or Mr Sand, say it's safe to uncover. Is that clear?'

Tizzie and the other *Questers* all nodded to show they had understood.

They then wasted no time in linking arms to go back through the Crystal Door.

This time, Mr Sand led the way, putting his hand on the green crystal before saying their destination.

'Pengtown, South Pole, Blizzardland, Acitcratna.'

NINETEEN

Caped Cavalry

CLPCLPCLPCLP. CLPCLPCLPCLP.

Behind the carts came men on horses.

The Imperial Guard Cavalry.

Louis watched as they all clip-clopped past.

CLPCLPCLPCLP. CLPCLPCLPCLP.

The riders all wore long red capes, which draped down over the backs of their horses.

Each cape had a large Evstika motif emblazoned on it.

Each rider was armed with a pistol, a long spear, and a long, thin sword. At intervals of one hundred riders, a centurion in a helmet with a red plume carried a huge Evstika flag.

CLPCLPCLPCLP. CLPCLPCLPCLP.

The cavalry took ages to ride past Louis, but they were finally gone.

Rrmmblrrmmblrrmmblrrmmbl...

Phew. He wasn't quite sure why – since he was still upsified on a post in a strange land with little chance of escape – but Louis nevertheless breathed a huge sigh of relief as the Emperor's entourage rumbled off into the distance.

Sqik. Sqik. Sqik. Sqik.

However, his relief was short-lived.

Because he now heard a familiar squeaky wheel heading in his direction from behind a hill along the road.

Sqik. Sqik. Sqik. Sqik.

TWENTY

Pengtown

The *Questers* arrived in the freezing South Pole, about two hundred paces from what Tizzie assumed must be Pengtown.

The town was a collection of very small houses, which looked as if they were made of snow and ice.

A snow storm was blowing, which made it very difficult to make things out, especially since everything here seemed to be some shade of white or grey.

From a distance, she could just about see that there were tiny little figures waddling about.

'Pengpeople!' exclaimed Jack, very close to her ear to make himself heard. 'I've always wanted to meet one.'

Tizzie simply nodded, so as not to give away the fact that she had no idea what a Pengperson was.

She decided to just watch, listen, and learn as they slowly made their way through the storm towards the town.

TWENTY-ONE

The Dastardly Duo

Sqik. Sqik. Sqik. Sqik.

Louis was sure it was the same squeaky wheel that had kept him awake during that first stormy night on the scary journey to the Polperro Inn.

Plumper confirmed his fears as a cart came into view along the road.

'Oh, nohh. It's Mr Drym... and he's got Spikey. And Scurvy's with him.'

'Oh, nohh,' moaned Louis, echoing Plumper as a worry-thought came straight to the front of his mind.

Has Mr Scurvy come for my teeth?

But the fears and concerns of boy and gnome were nothing compared to those of their canine companion.

'Ueww. Uewww. Ueww. Uewwwwwwwwwww.'

Dribble whined pitifully and wriggled on his post in a desperate attempt to free himself as the dastardly duo approached.

TWENTY-TWO

Pengpeople

Clevercloggs led the way as the *Questers* arrived at the outskirts of Pengtown. Through the blizzard, Tizzie saw that it was more like a village than a town. There were only a few hundred of the snowhouses, each situated a few paces apart from the others in a seemingly random pattern.

It was now that she noticed a number of Pengpeople waddling towards them. It was still hard to see them clearly because of the snowstorm but she could just make out that they had patches of dark black and bright white feathers all over their bodies, just like penguins. Yet they had faces and hands and feet like humans. And they didn't seem to feel the cold. They must be mutants, decided Tizzie.

As the Pengpeople came closer, she saw they were all carrying long poles with barbed, bone hooks on the end, which made her worry that they might not be friendly. But it was quickly evident that the Pengpeople were not going to hurt them, and the *Questers* were soon being escorted towards the largest snowhouse.

There was no door at the entrance to the dwelling, just a long, tunnel-like, porchway. The little gnome walked straight in as if it were his own home. The other *Questers* followed him down the tunnel porchway.

Inside, there was a very aged Pengperson.

He recognised his surprise visitor instantly.

'Hello Clevercloggs, old friend.'

TWENTY-THREE

I'm Going To Die

Drym and Scurvy were sitting in the front of the first gaol cart in a procession of gaol carts.

This first cart drove past all the other upsified prisoners until it came to the very end of the road before the bridge.

'UEWW. UEWWWW.'

Dribble whined louder as the cart came to a halt in the middle of the road, right between Louis and Plumper.

Louis heard the little dog's thoughts in his head.

'*Drym's going to kill me. I'm going to die.*'

For a moment, he felt so sorry for Dribble that it made him forget his own fear. Then Scurvy spoke and Louis remembered that these two men were as nasty as any he'd ever met.

And one of them wanted his teeth.

'Well, well, well. If it isn't the boy with the gleaming teeth. I'm going to have those teeth, Mr Drym. A nice set of new ones to soothe my bleeding gums.'

'You deserve them, Mr Scurvy, for all your hard work. Oh yes you do,' said Drym. 'Such a shame that the King's instructions are that no harm is to come to any of the prisoners *before* the Games, oh yes it is.

'Otherwise, I'd ask Spikey to kill that fat little gnome.

'And I'd have Danglefang devour that drooling, good-for-nothing mutt...

'RIGHT HERE! RIGHT NOW! OH YES I WOULD!'

TWENTY-FOUR

Chief Guin

Chief Guin was the leader of the Pengpeople.

He and Clevercloggs had a good talk, during which Clevercloggs explained how the *Questers* were searching the continents for the Rainbow Crystals for the *Amulet of Hope* and that they needed help in the forthcoming uprising against Evile.

Guin agreed to help and said he would spread the word amongst the other Peng who lived throughout Acitcratna.

'That's marvellous, thank you for your help,' said Clevercloggs.

'Now we need to find the Orange Rainbow Crystal.

'Godolphin's map says it's here in Pengtown.'

'Oh, I know where that will be,' said Chief Guin.

'We've got lots of orange crystals.

'They're over here.'

With that, he turned and slowly waddle-walked towards the back wall of the snowhouse.

TWENTY-FIVE

Gaol Carts

At the mention of his name, Danglefang stirred from his lying down position in the gaol cart and growled menacingly.

'RRRRRRRRRRRRR.'

Louis stared in awe at the wolfspider as it slowly rose up on to its eight hairy legs.

'RRRRRRRRRRRRRRRRRRRRRRRRRRRRRRRR.'

Danglefang continued to growl menacingly as Drym let him out of the cart.

'UEWW. UEWWWW.'

Little Dribble whimpered and whined ever more frantically as Drym and Scurvy lowered the prisoners down from their posts.

Soon Louis was lying by the side of the road with Dribble, Plumper, and seven more little people.

'We're all gnomes from the same village,' said Plumper to Louis.

He then pointed around the group as he introduced everyone.

'This is Longlegs, Fishalot, Greenfingers, Flowerpot, Seesaw, Swinger, and that's Prickle.

'We're all friends but they're going to make us fight each other in the Colosseum.'

'That's not nice,' said Louis. 'I've got to fight as well. But I don't want to either.' Then he leaned forward and whispered: 'Do you think we should try to escape now?'

Clnk. Clnk. Clnk. Clnk.

Before anyone had a chance to answer, Drym and Scurvy had walked back and clasped rusty old shackles around their ankles.

The prisoners were hauled to their feet.

Louis knew he had missed his chance to escape.

He could barely walk with the shackles on, let alone run.

It was then that Danglefang began to round them up.

'Rrrrrrrrrrrrrrrrr.'

The growling wolfspider herded them in the direction of Drym's gaol cart.

All the other upsified prisoners along the road were also put into carts.

When they were loaded with their pitiful cargo, all the carts turned in the opposite direction to the way they had come and started back along the road into Wonrekland.

Louis, Dribble, and the eight gnomes, were now in the last cart in the procession.

'Ueww. Uewww.'

Flowerpot was stroking Dribble's back, doing what she could to comfort the distraught little dog.

Louis asked Plumper the question that was on everybody's mind.

'Do you know where they're taking us?'

'I overheard one of the guards saying that all of us prisoners will be going straight for training as gladiators...

'...to the Conquest Colosseum.'

TWENTY-SIX

The Second Rainbow Crystal: Orange

On the back wall inside Chief Guin's snowhouse there was a big square lump of snow rising from ground level to about Tizzie's knee height.

Guin started scraping the top of the snow square with his tiny but strong hands. After a few moments of scraping, there, lying on the snow, were at least fifty orange crystals, all exactly the same shape and size.

'These are the crystals that Godolphin left here with the ancestors for safe-keeping,' said Guin. 'The story handed down through the generations is that he left so many to disguise the one that belongs in the *Amulet*.'

'I don't think that will be a prob...,' began Clevercloggs.

Before he could even finish his sentence, what he was going to say had been confirmed. One of the crystals shot a laser of orange light out at Jack.

'Well, well,' said Chief Guin. 'I'd imagine this young man is a Rainbow Wizard.'

'Then you'd imagine correctly,' said Clevercloggs with a big smile.

The leader of the Pengpeople went to retrieve the Second Crystal of the *Amulet* from the pile.

'I wouldn't do tha...' began Mr Sand.

'Ow!' exclaimed Chief Guin, as he dropped the crystal, 'it's *hot*!'

'I was trying to say I think it will only be Jack who can retrieve the crystal from the pile,' said Mr Sand.

He then beckoned Jack to step forward.

Jack moved into position just in front of the square of snow.

Kneeling down, he pointed his wand and said, 'orange stone come here', in Kernewek.

'*Men owraval omma dos.*'

The stone jumped from the pile and landed in his open palm.

In this way, by using his wand, Jack was able to retrieve the Orange Crystal without getting burnt. Once he had done so, he put the crystal in the pouch around his neck for safe-keeping.

The *Questers* thanked Chief Guin and said their goodbyes.

Once they had all walked back to the edge of Pengtown and lined up with their hands on each other's shoulders as before, Clevercloggs bent down, put the crystal end of the Golden Key on the ground… and said the words to make it work.

'*Golden Cavern, by the power of Godolphin.*'

The *Questers* disappeared into the snow.

TWENTY-SEVEN

Uhccip Uhcam, Acirema South

The *Questers* arrived back in the Golden Cavern.

The Godolphin Map was already in Mr Sand's hand.

He gave it to Jack.

The apprentice pointed his Red Wand at the map.

He spoke in his special spell voice.

'*Golow an mappa.*'

Tizzie and the others watched as a point of yellow light began to glow faintly on the map.

The yellow light started to blink.

It was blinking in Acirema South.

Tizzie tried to read the words on the map.

'Uhccip Uhcam in Urep,' said Mr Sand, with a glance at Clevercloggs.

'Very remote,' said Clevercloggs. 'High in the mountains. Another good place to hide something important. And it means we can speak to King Pachacuti, the leader of the Incas.

'If we can convince him to join the rebellion, many of the good people of Acirema South will surely follow his lead.'

They wasted no time in linking arms to go back through the Crystal Door.

Mr Sand was at the front. He said their destination.

'Uhccip Uhcam, Urep, Mountainland, Acirema South.'

As it softened, the *Questers* stepped into the green crystal.

TWENTY-EIGHT

What I Want

Evile's entourage was nearing Wonrek Castle. Inside the purple-draped carriage, the Emperor was looking at a scroll of parchment. It had '*What I Want*' written along the top.

The Emperor had a very acquisitive personality, which meant that he was never satisfied with what he had. He always wanted more and more... and then still more.

In the case of this territory, he wanted lots of things. As usual, he wanted so much that, in order to remember everything, he had made his list. He had put a line through some of the things on the list because they had been achieved.

Surveying his list, the Emperor was very pleased that he had already been able to achieve so many things he wanted.

He'd only put a line through half of the 'Build the Conquest Colosseum' item because it wasn't finished.

In regard to those items that did not yet have a line through them, Evile was sure it would only be a matter of time before Professor Mullion gave in and told all he knew about the technology like zooming maps, eyes in the skies, eelectricity, and so on.

Manaccan leaned over ever-so-slightly to try to catch a glimpse of the list.

Evile noticed and very quickly folded it up towards his chin so that his underling couldn't see the second item on the parchment.

What I Want

~~Conquer Kernowland~~

~~Install a puppet king~~

~~Change name to Wonrekland~~

~~Impose Martial Law~~

~~Establish and Enforce Edicts I-to X~~

~~Set up Imperial Tax System~~

~~Capture Professor Mullion~~

Zooming Maps and Space Orbiters

Eelectricity

Golden Key and Crystal Door

Godolphin Map

~~Build the Conquest~~ Colosseum

Gladiator Games

TWENTY-NINE

Professor Mullion's Dilemma

Professor Mullion had a huge dilemma. He was being held in the dungeons at the castle and had very quickly learned why he was a prisoner. The Emperor wanted Kernowland's advanced technology – eyes in the skies, zooming maps, eelectricity – and Mullion was the expert on them all. It had come as a shock to the professor that his colleague, Dr Lizard, was a traitor who had told King Manaccan that Mullion had recently discovered a way to reproduce the Golden Key, so that lots more people could use Godolphin's system of instant travel from – and back to – the Golden Cavern.

Professor Mullion was a good man. He didn't want to help these bad people. But Mr Lister had taken great care to list all the nasty things that would be done to his wife and children if he didn't cooperate; including selling his children into slavery and making his wife fight for her life in the Colosseum. Lister had written all these things down in big letters and pinned the list on a wall opposite the cell door… so that Mullion could see it *all* the time. The poor professor had gone over and over the list, getting more and more worried for his family every time he read it. He was being given a clear choice. Either he could help the new regime with his scientific brilliance. Or, the things on Lister's list would be done to his family.

In the end, he simply had no choice. He had to give in and help King Manaccan and the Emperor.

For the sake of his wife and little children.

THIRTY

The Temple Of The Sun

The *Questers* arrived in Urep on the side of a mountain.

They could see a walled city above them.

'The famous, Uhccip Uhcam,' said Clevercloggs.

'Magnificent,' said Princess Kea.

Tizzie had to agree. It was a wonderful sight. The mountains surrounding the city were spectacular.

They climbed the steep mountainside.

At the gate they were challenged by the guards.

Clevercloggs introduced himself and, luckily, the uncle of one of the guards knew the old gnome from shared adventures long ago.

They were taken to see King Pachacuti.

The King knew Clevercloggs well because the little gnome had helped him solve an irrigation problem many years before.

He welcomed the *Questers* warmly, and listened carefully as Clevercloggs explained their quest for the Eight Crystals of the famous *Amulet of Hope* and the plans for a wurldwide rebellion.

The King understood that the plan depended on an uprising of all the good people at once. He agreed to form a 'RAE Force of Acirema South', which would join in the wurldwide RAE Rebellion when the time came.

But for now, it was time to find the Yellow Crystal.

They zoomed in on the Godolphin Map.

'It's showing us the stone is in the Temple of the Sun.'

THIRTY-ONE

Darkness Beneath The Colosseum

The gaol carts arrived at their destination.

The prisoners were forced out of the carts.

They were marched down steps, along dark corridors, and then thrown into dimly lit cells beneath the Colosseum.

'I bet they're going to keep us here and only let us out for training and the actual fighting,' said Prickle.

Louis learned from the gnomes that there were all sorts of prisoners being held in the underground cells who were going to be made to fight.

They included teachers, soldiers, rebels, troublemakers, and anyone else Mr Scurvy had decided should be imprisoned.

On the very first night, Drym came down into the cells.

He was accompanied by Danglefang.

'RRRRRRRRRRRRRRRR.'

The Slaver-in-Chief went straight up to the bars of Dribble's cell and began dropping red slabs of meat on the stone floor, so that the shaking little dog could see.

Sqlch. Mnch.

'Uewww. Uewwww. Uewwww.'

Dribble whimpered and whined as he watched the wolfspider devour the slabs of meat in seconds.

Drym pointed Spikey at the terrified little dachshund.

'You're the next lump of red meat on his menu, slobberdog.

'OH, YES YOU ARE!'

46

THIRTY-TWO

The Third Rainbow Crystal: Yellow

The *Questers* followed the King to the Temple of the Sun.

Once in the Temple, Tizzie saw an amazing sight: the dazzling Crown Jewels of the Incas.

There were a huge number of glistening stones in the Crown Jewels, including lots of yellow crystals.

'If we didn't have a Rainbow Wizard, it would be like looking for a needle in a haystack!' said Mr Sand.

Suddenly, a thin beam of yellow light shot like a laser from one of the crystals set in the Crown of Mountainland.

The laser emanating from the Crown shone onto Jack's chest, creating a little yellow dot right over his heart.

'It's found you again,' said Clevercloggs. 'May we have it for the *Amulet*, King Pachacuti?'

'Of course, the Inca people would be proud to help.'

With that, the King attempted to remove the Yellow Rainbow Crystal from its mounting in the Crown with his fingers.

'Noh...' Clevercloggs tried to stop him.

ZZZZZZZZZ!

Tizzie winced as the stone gave the King something like an electric shock. He immediately let go of it and fell backwards.

'Are you all right?' said Princess Kea, as she helped the King to his feet.

'Wow, that crystal certainly packs a punch,' said Clevercloggs. 'Jack, we'll need you to use your magic.'

With that, he held out the Crown in front of the teenager.

Jack pointed his wand and said, 'yellow stone come here', in Kernewek.

'*Men melyn omma dos.*'

The crystal popped out into his hand.

'Great effort, you've done it again,' said Mr Sand.

The *Questers* thanked King Pachacuti and said their goodbyes.

Tizzie would have liked to stay longer at the Temple of the Sun but she knew they were in a hurry.

They were soon all lining up with their hands on each other's shoulders as before.

Tizzie readied herself as Clevercloggs bent down and put the crystal end of the Golden Key on the ground and uttered the now familiar words to make it work: '*Golden Cavern, by the power of Godolphin.*'

THIRTY-THREE

Og

Louis was in a cell opposite the gnomes.

He was exhausted and had his eyes closed, trying to get some sleep before what he had been told would be a long session of gruelling gladiator training the next day.

The gnomes were whispering but he could hear what they were saying.

His new friends were talking about his opponent… Og.

They obviously thought Louis was asleep.

'I feel so sorry for that little prince,' said Greenfingers. 'He has to fight that horrible creature who smashes everything up with his big ironhammer.'

'Does anyone know anything else about Og?' asked Flowerpot.

'Yes,' said Plumper, 'Clevercloggs told me all about him.'

'Tell us,' said the other gnomes all at once as they gathered round their fat friend.

Plumper told what he knew about the Ogreman in an even lower whisper as Louis pretended to sleep.

'Ogres live in Fjordland, the home of the Vikings.

'But Og is special. A mutant.

'He *is* an ogre, but he's *also* part human; which means he's much cleverer than other ogres.'

Louis could still just hear what was being said. He listened with increasing dread as Plumper continued.

'Og, wasn't born. He was hatched from an ogre-egg. Ogre mothers lay their eggs in denburrows, which are like rabbit holes but much bigger. This means the eggs are buried deep in the ground. Og's mother laid her egg and then covered the entrance to the denburrow with a boulder to protect it. Her mothering job now done, she left Og to hatch on his own.

'Ogre hatchlings are called "ogretts". Like all ogretts, Og was immediately strong enough to move the boulder and could look after himself as soon as he left the denburrow.

'Og grew to be taller than two tall Viking men. He learned to become a fearsome hunter. His main prey was reindeer. But he occasionally took human food. In time, he developed a real taste for it, especially child-meat.

'Hrappr Bloodaxe heard about the Ogreman who was eating children. The Vikings caught him in a trap and he was made into a gladiator. In no time at all, Og had killed over one hundred people, animals, and creatures in the colosseums of the Empire. His fame quickly spread. He became the Emperor's Champion. But his fights aren't really contests... they're *slaughters*. The crowd loves the way he takes his time as he toys with his opponents... smashing them up bit by bit with his ironhammer. And, in a few days... he'll be facing his two-hundredth victim.'

As he spoke, Plumper turned his head towards Louis' cell.

All the other gnomes did the same.

'Poor Prince Louis,' said Flowerpot.

Louis was still pretending to be asleep, but he had heard every word. Now he couldn't sleep. As the night wore on, he tried to think of something else. Anything else. But one fearful word was going around and around in his head.

'*Ironhammer... Ironhammer... Ironhammer.*'

THIRTY-FOUR

Ololoolo

The *Questers* were soon back in the Golden Cavern.

They looked at the Godolphin Map for their next destination. Jack pointed his wand.

'*Golow an mappa.*'

A green light began blinking on the map.

Tizzie watched and listened as Jack said: 'It's showing the crystal is in a place called Ololoolo in Savannahland. That's where Masai said he came from.'

'I know that place,' said Clevercloggs, 'it's near the Aram River.

'We'll need to change clothes again to go there.'

Then he said, 'Ololoolo, Aram Aisam, Savannahland,' before opening the rucksack again and pulling out some garments that looked like they were suitable for a safari.

'The rest of us need to go back through the Traveller's Tunnel,' said Mr Sand.

They all did as instructed.

After walking through the tunnel again, even though Tizzie knew what to expect, she was nonetheless amazed that she came out with safari clothes on.

When everyone had been through the Traveller's Tunnel, Clevercloggs spoke in a very serious tone.

'Acirfa is full of wild, dangerous, and ferocious animals, mutants, and Chewing Creatures. We'll need to be on constant guard and keep our weapons ready.'

This reminded Tizzie of her experience with Big Red Grunter in Jungleland. She hoped they wouldn't meet any more Chewing Creatures like that giant boarmonster.

The *Questers* then wasted no time in linking arms to go back through the Crystal Door.

This time, Clevercloggs led the way, putting his hand on the door before saying their destination.

'Ololoolo Camp, Aram Aisam, Aynek, Savannahland, Acirfa.'

THIRTY-FIVE

Rudarius

The prisoners were dragged in chains from their cells beneath the Colosseum and marched up some steps.

After being in the dark for so long, it took a little while for Louis' eyes to get used to the glare of the sun. He then saw a tall man holding a short sword standing in front of them.

'He's huge,' whispered Louis to Plumper.

'He's the trainer,' said Plumper.

The trainer introduced himself.

'I am Rudarius.'

They learned that Rudarius was a former gladiator who had won his freedom by being the victor in many contests in the colosseums of the Empire.

'You will listen carefully and learn quickly,' continued Rudarius. 'Your lives depend on it... and I mean that literally.'

Louis, Plumper, and all the other prisoners, now straightened their backs, pricked up their ears, and gave the trainer their undivided attention.

'Good, now we can begin,' said Rudarius. 'All the words used in things to do with colosseums come from Nital, the ancient language of Emor. The Conquest Colosseum is an *arena*. In Nital, that word means *sandy place*.'

Louis glanced around the vast Colosseum and saw that the entire wooden floor of the arena was covered in a deep layer of sand.

THIRTY-SIX

Chief Olonana

The *Questers* arrived on an escarpment overlooking the Ololoolo Camp. The Aram River ran alongside the Camp, serving the people's water needs.

'These are the Maasai people,' said Clevercloggs on the way down to the Camp. 'They are very proud and fearsome warriors. They can run for many hours at a time across Savannahland in search of their food. When the boys become teenagers, they have to fight a lion with only a spear to prove they are men. I hope Chief Olonana is there. He is a good man, and his brave fighters, called *morans*, will be great allies in the uprising against Evile.'

The Ololoolo Camp was comprised of thousands of circular houses.

'They call their dwellings *manyattas*,' informed Mr Sand. 'They're made by the women and constructed from mud and cow dung.'

The Camp compound was surrounded by a double-thickness, very high, wooden fence.

'That fence keeps their cattle in and the carnivorous beasts and Chewing Creatures out,' said Clevercloggs.

Hearing this, Tizzie thought it might be a good idea to get inside the fence as soon as possible. She quickened her step.

When they reached the Camp gate, Clevercloggs was immediately recognised and they were taken to see Chief Olonana.

THIRTY-SEVEN

SMSH! SMSH! SMSH!

'The Nital word for *sword* is *gladius*,' said Rudarius as he held his short sword aloft for everyone to see. 'And, from that, we get the name, *gladiator*... or *swordsman*.

'But gladiators do not just use these short swords.

'There are all sorts of gladiators who use all sorts of different weapons, such as the war chain, the net, the trident, the club, the dagger, and the lasso.

'Some of you will use two swords, some long swords, others will use scissor-swords.

'For protection, some of you will have a shield. Others will have a helmet, or a patch of leather, or piece of cloth guarding a part of their body.

'Each type of gladiator has a special name.

'We will decide which type of gladiator you are going to be, depending on your size and your skills.

'Some of you will ride horses, others will be charioteers.

'Some of you will be trained to fight the carnivorous beasts of Erthwurld.

'And those of you who have incurred the wrath of the Emperor will be fed to the Chewing Creatures. You will need no training for this.'

Louis soon learned that he was to fight with a gladius and shield.

The young boy was made to practise and practise and practise throughout the day.

He had to hit a wooden post with his sword over and over again.

He had to run and jump and do exercises to build up his muscles.

The shield was heavy but he had to learn how to hold it up to protect himself.

At the end of the first day's training, as he was leaving, an exhausted Louis saw Og come in to the arena.

Everyone stopped to look.

SMSH! SMSH! SMSH!

The Ogreman began his training by smashing up slabs of rock with his Ironhammer.

Plumper and the other gnomes looked first at Og and then at Louis.

The trembling young boy could sense they were all feeling the same thing.

They pitied him.

It was easy to see why.

Og was gigantic; the Emperor's Champion.

He was a tiny boy.

It was obvious to everyone what was going to happen when little Louis met the giant Og in the Conquest Colosseum.

THIRTY-EIGHT

Your Brave Son Is Alive

'My warriors and I are ready to help in whatever way we can,' said Chief Olonana, when he learned of RAE's plans for the uprising. 'The sooner we can rid Erthwurld of that terrible tyrant and his allies, the better.'

Then the Chief's mood saddened as he added. 'If only my own son, Masai, were here to take part in the battle. But I am afraid that will not be possible. He went out alone, to prove himself a man, with just a spear to fight a lion. But he didn't come back.'

Jack was now very glad to be able to say what he knew. 'I'm happy to tell you that your son didn't die fighting a lion, Chief Olonana. The slavers kidnapped him whilst he was asleep and sold him to Pigleg the Pirate.'

'Oh, I see,' said the Chief, now looking even more sad. 'So he's a slave. That is worse than death for a moran warrior.'

'But that's not the full story,' added Clevercloggs quickly. 'Your son has escaped and has shown great courage. He saved the life of Princess Tizzie here by diving into a shoal of piranhasharks, losing a toe in the process. And he is, at this very moment, escorting the younger children who escaped with him to safety.'

'Then my son was brave?'

'Very brave indeed.'

The Chief beamed.

He seemed very happy to hear this news.

THIRTY-NINE

A Visit By Godolphin

Clevercloggs now told Chief Olonana of their quest for the crystals.

'Godolphin's Map shows us that the Green Crystal we seek is in the Camp compound,' said Clevercloggs.

'That is correct,' said the Chief. 'Our people have long told a story of a visit by Godolphin the Great.

'He came to our tribe and left a green shining stone for safe-keeping with my ancestor, Lenana the Brave.

'We agreed to keep the stone until a good magician came to collect it.

'Godolphin said the crystal was only to be released to one chosen by the stone.

'But it was never made clear what that meant.'

'I think that it will soon become clear,' said Mr Sand, with a smile in Jack's direction.

'Yes,' said Clevercloggs, 'if you could take us to the stone, as my friend says, you may get the answer very quickly.'

'We need to go to the Temple Hut,' said the Chief.

Tizzie was soon trudging through the mud with the other *Questers* as Chief Olonana led them towards the biggest building in the Camp.

FORTY

The Fourth Rainbow Crystal: Green

As they approached the Temple Hut, Tizzie could see it was guarded by two very tall warriors with long, sharp spears.

The Chief and the *Questers* went inside.

Tizzie saw a large wooden box on an altar.

Chief Olonana opened the box.

A green glow emanated from within.

Everyone took a step closer and looked at its contents.

Sure enough, inside, as expected, was a green crystal.

It was sitting on a metal stand and was obviously the source of the glow.

'It would certainly seem that each crystal has different properties,' said Mr Sand to the other *Questers*.

'Yes, I agree,' said Clevercloggs. 'But, fortunately, that is not our current concern. All we need know is that, when set together in the *Amulet*, the Seven Rainbow Crystals will enhance the power of *Photos* in any battle against *Skotos*.'

Chief Olonana now spoke very seriously.

'As I said, my people agreed that we would only release the Green Crystal to one chosen by the gem stone itself. Is one of you a Rainbow Wiz...'

Before the Chief could finish, a green laser beam shot from the crystal and hit Jack in the heart, just as the red, orange, and yellow stones had done.

Acting on a nod from Clevercloggs, Jack stepped forward

and pointed his wand, at the same time saying, 'green stone come here', in Kernewek.

'*Men gwyrdh omma dos.*'

Tizzie watched in awe as the stone rose slowly from its metal support and floated into Jack's open hand.

The Chief smiled as if he were very pleased.

'So, it really *has* begun.

'I wish you well in the remainder of your task.

'As I said before, when the time comes, you can rely on the moran warriors of Savannahland.

'We will be ready to help in the fight against the Tyrant.'

The *Questers* thanked Chief Olonana again.

He said goodbye before leaving them alone in the Temple Hut.

Once they had all lined up with their hands on each other's shoulders, Clevercloggs bent down and put the crystal end of the Golden Key on the floor of the hut.

'*Golden Cavern, by the power of Godolphin.*'

FORTY-ONE

Horseback Fighters Of The Arena

Louis was back in the arena the next day for more arduous training.

During a rest period, he was able to watch the horseback fighters practising. Rudarius explained that there were different types of horseback fighters.

One type, the *Andabatae*, wore chain mail. Louis was amazed to see that they also wore helmets *without* eye holes. He watched as two men charged at one another on horseback, just like in a joust... but without being able to see each other!

Other horseback fighters were the *Sagittarii*. Each of these men was armed with a bow which could fire an arrow over a great distance. Louis was impressed that they could hit the bulls-eyes on targets as they galloped past at great speed.

Yet other horsemen were called *Equites*. They wore armour and a brimmed helmet with two decorative feathers sticking out of it. They carried a round cavalry shield, and had an arm-guard, called a *manica*, on their right arm.

As Louis watched the horseback fighters training, Rudarius said: 'As you can see, the Equites ride white horses. They will be on the Programme of Dread on the opening day of the Gladiator Games. They start on horseback, but once they have thrown their *hasta* lance, they dismount and continue to fight on foot with their gladius. The crowd love the Equites. They will cheer loudly when the white horses enter the Conquest Colosseum.'

FORTY-TWO

Uluru

The *Questers* were soon back in the Golden Cavern. They opened the Godolphin Map to discover their next destination.

Jack pointed his wand: '*Golow an mappa.*'

A blue light began blinking on the map.

Tizzie watched and listened as Princess Kea exclaimed: 'Uluru! The Red Rock.'

As before, Clevercloggs wasted no time in getting ready for the next journey. He said: 'Uluru, Araluy, Dustland, Ailartsua,' before opening his rucksack again and pulling out suitable garments.

Very soon, Tizzie and the rest of the *Questers* had each been through the Traveller's Tunnel. This time, as well as suitable clothes, the tunnel had also provided them all with a large pouch filled with fresh water that hung diagonally across their backs, supported by a thick piece of string across their fronts. Everyone was now ready to go.

Mr Sand spoke: 'The part of Ailartsua we're going to is very hot, and dry, and dusty. People who are not used to the heat can dehydrate and collapse and die very quickly. So make sure you drink plenty of water at regular intervals.'

Tizzie made a mental note to drink lots of water.

The *Questers* then linked arms to go back through the Crystal Door. Clevercloggs again led the way, putting his hand on the green crystal before saying their destination.

'Uluru, Araluy, Dustland, Ailartsua.'

FORTY-THREE

Chief Kata Of The Anangu

The *Questers* arrived a few hundred paces away from Uluru. As they approached the huge red rock, Mr Sand told them some things about it.

'Uluru is an inselberg. It's made of a coarse sandstone called *arkos*.'

'What's an inselberg?' asked Tizzie.

'It means *island mountain*,' answered Mr Sand before continuing. 'The rock rises nearly twelve hundred feet above the desert. Two-thirds of the inselberg is underground. It is three-and-a-half kiloms in length and two-and-a-half kiloms wide. Its base is nearly ten kiloms in circumference. It appears to change colour at different times of the day and at different times of the year. When it rains, the rock turns silver-grey. At sunset, it glows red.'

Tizzie looked up at Uluru in wonderment as they approached. After what Mr Sand had said, she imagined it as a rocky red iceberg rising from a sea of sand.

A group of Blackskin men and women were sitting in a circle at the base of the huge rock.

'They're the Anangu Tribe,' said Clevercloggs. 'I know their leader, Chief Kata.'

As soon as they saw the strangers, eight warriors grabbed their woomeras, spears, and boomerangs, and ran towards the *Questers*, ready to defend their tribe.

But, as they came closer, the warriors soon recognised Clevercloggs. They quickly lowered their weapons and surrounded their old friend with big smiles and warm greetings.

Clevercloggs and the other *Questers* were welcomed into the Anangu circle and the little gnome was soon in conversation with Chief Kata.

Tizzie listened intently as they talked.

'Yes, the Great Wizard from your land was here,' said Kata. 'He left a blue gem stone with the ancestors for safekeeping.'

'Is it still safe?' asked Mr Sand.

'It is indeed,' answered the Chief. 'It is in a crevice near the top of the Sacred Rock. I will send one of my warriors to fetch it.'

'I don't think that will be possible,' said Clevercloggs. 'You see, we have reason to believe that the stones of the *Amulet* protect themselves in different ways. It appears that only a Rainbow Wizard can handle them.'

'I see no wizard,' said Chief Kata, looking around the group of *Questers* before him.

Clevercloggs moved his eyes towards Jack.

'Ah, I see,' said Chief Kata, with a sceptical look on his face. 'An apprentice?'

'Yes,' said Clevercloggs. 'But he has proven himself worthy of collecting the first four stones, so we have no reason to suppose that he will not be able to retrieve this next one.'

'Well, young man, it appears that you have sufficient skills in wizardry to handle Godolphin's special stones,' said the Chief, now apparently much more impressed as he looked directly at Jack.

'But can you climb Uluru?'

FORTY-FOUR

The Noxii

Louis was training again.

He had learned that he was in a category of combatants called, *Noxii*. Rudarius had said this word meant, 'criminal fighters'. All the teachers, soldiers, rebels, and troublemakers were in the same group as him.

The crowd hated condemned criminals who fought in the Colosseum, and they loved to see the Noxii have as hard a time as possible in the arena.

When a pair of Noxii was matched, each was given a disadvantage to excite the crowd.

Sometimes, one criminal had a weapon, but was blindfolded, whilst the other had no weapon, but could see.

In the contest between Plumper and Longlegs, the fat gnome had just learned that he would be the blindfolded one.

'I just don't know if I can hurt Longlegs,' he said. 'He's my best friend.'

Louis could understand that.

He didn't know if he could hurt one of his friends if they were forced to fight in the Colosseum.

In fact, he wondered if he could hurt anyone at all.

Even if his own life depended on it.

FORTY-FIVE

Dont Look Down!

'Godolphin wanted to put the blue stone in a very safe place,' said Chief Kata. 'So he put it up there.'

Tizzie strained her neck to look up to where he was pointing. The crystal had obviously been left on a very steep and sheer part of the rock, almost at the top.

She was standing next to Jack.

'Be careful,' she said to her friend as she looked up at the almost vertical climb ahead of him. 'It looks very dangerous. Are you scared?'

'Yes, I am actually,' said Jack. 'But I've got to do it. We must have all seven of the crystals.'

Chief Kata had decided to personally help Jack recover the crystal.

'Follow every move I make as exactly as you can,' said the Chief, as he planted a foot and grabbed an outcrop of rock.

'And, whatever you do when climbing, never look down!'

Tizzie, who was a little scared of heights, thought this was very good advice. Jack simply nodded and put his left foot on the rock just where Chief Kata had put his a few moments earlier. Then he grabbed the same outcrop and pulled himself up to begin the climb.

'Good luck,' said Tizzie, 'and please be careful.'

She then heard Mr Sand whisper to Clevercloggs behind her as he too looked up at the near vertical rock face.

'I think that boy's going to need all the luck he can get.'

FORTY-SIX

A Big Mistake

Jack followed Chief Kata's every move for half of the climb.

But, when they stopped for a break to rest their aching arms and legs, he completely forgot the Chief's advice.

He looked down!

This was a big mistake.

Suddenly his head was spinning.

He released his grip.

He could feel himself falling backwards from the rock.

'Ahhhhhhhhh!'

The young apprentice cried out as he started dropping towards the ground.

Down below, Tizzie watched what was happening to her friend.

She screamed as Jack fell backwards.

'Nohhhhhhhhhhhh!'

FORTY-SEVEN

Tggg!

Tggg!

Jack felt the tug of the rope that joined him by his waist to Chief Kata. Looking skyward, he saw that the Chief had gripped the rock tightly and was desperately shifting his feet to get the firmest footing he could.

Jack was just dangling helplessly in mid-air. The only things saving him from certain death were the fingers and feet of Chief Kata.

Luckily, the Chief was incredibly strong and twice Jack's weight. He shouted down to the young wizard whose life depended on what they both did next.

'I have a secure footing, Jack. I'll try to swing you towards the rock. As soon as you get near enough, grab on tightly.'

'Okay,' said Jack from below.

'Pfff!'

Moments later, the teenager had the wind knocked out of him as he smashed into the red rock, grazing both his knees badly as he did so. But he somehow managed to hold on tightly and secure his footing.

'Phew.' He sighed with relief. Tizzie did the same below.

'Now, what *mustn't* you do?' shouted Chief Kata from above.

'I mustn't look down,' said Jack.

'That's right!' said the Chief, smiling with a mixture of warmth and relief as they began climbing once more.

FORTY-EIGHT

The Fifth Rainbow Crystal: Blue

When Jack and Chief Kata had nearly reached the top of Uluru, they stopped either side of a little crevice, both of them holding on securely with their fingers and feet.

Deep inside the crevice, Jack could see the Blue Crystal. The gap was not wide enough to get a hand in, let alone a whole arm.

'Godolphin certainly hid this one well!' said Chief Kata. 'Looks like we'll need a branch or something to ge...'

Before the Chief could finish his sentence, a blue laser beam suddenly shot from the stone and shone on Jack's heart.

Chief Kata seemed impressed.

'You're obviously the one to collect it!'

Holding on even more tightly with his left hand, the young apprentice now withdrew his Red Wand with his right.

Pointing at the crystal, he said, 'blue stone come here', in Kernewek: '*Men glas omma dos.*'

The stone jiggled about inside the crevice until it was loose and then began rolling out towards the young apprentice.

With his wand in his right hand, and his left hand securing him to the rock, Jack wondered how on erth he was going to catch the crystal.

It looked like the stone was going to roll out and fall erthwards. They both realised it could be lost.

Suddenly Chief Kata acted and grabbed Jack's right arm.

'I've got you. Catch it.'

Feeling the Chief's strong grip on his arm, Jack released his hold with his left hand and stretched to catch the Blue Rainbow Crystal as it rolled out of the crevice.

Plllpp.

The crystal plopped into his palm.

'Well done, young man,' said the Chief, smiling warmly once more. 'Godolphin would be proud of you.'

Jack beamed back at the Chief and they quickly began their descent.

When they had climbed safely back down to the ground, everyone was full of praise and admiration for both of them.

Whilst Jack sat down for a well-earned rest, Misty wasted no time in waggling his whiskers and healing the young wizard's grazed knees.

Clevercloggs then apologised that they would have to leave straight away as they had more crystals to find and very little time in which to do so.

'Both I and my warriors will be ready to rise up against the Empire of Evil when the time comes,' confirmed the Chief.

The *Questers* thanked Chief Kata for all his help and said their goodbyes.

They lined up at the dusty base of Uluru.

Clevercloggs bent down and put the crystal end of the Golden Key on the ground.

'*Golden Cavern, by the power of Godolphin.*'

FORTY-NINE

Chomp The Chewing Chihuahua

Louis was training once more.

There was a Chewing Creature in the middle of the arena.

It was Chomp the Chewing Chihuahua.

He knew from the Programme of Dread that Miss Prudent, the former headmistress of Towan Blystra Primary School – and good friend of Mr Sand's whom he'd met at the Banquet Ball – would be fighting Chomp.

Miss Prudent loved animals and had said to one of her friends that she wondered how she was going to fight a little dog without hurting it.

But she had obviously not actually *seen* Chomp the Chewing Chihuahua when she said this.

Because the creature Louis was looking at was at least as big as a lion.

It had six pointed fangs in its mouth.

And long sharp claws on its paws.

It was definitely no ordinary Chihuahua.

The Chewing Creature was tied to a post by a chain.

Trainers were baiting it with long pointed sticks.

Louis was standing next to his fat little friend.

'Why are they poking it like that, Plumper?'

'They're trying to make it more ferocious for the fight against Miss Prudent. It'll hate people by the time they've finished with it.'

Poor Miss Prudent, thought Louis, I wonder if she knows?

FIFTY

Iun Apar

Back in the Golden Cavern, the *Questers* looked at the Godolphin Map to discover their next destination.

Jack pointed his wand.

'*Golow an mappa.*'

An indigo light began blinking on the map.

Jack made Tizzie jump when he exclaimed loudly: 'Iun Apar… the *Island of Statues.*'

'Yes,' said Clevercloggs, 'and it's the most remote island in the wurld. A great place to hide the sixth crystal.'

They then wasted no time in getting ready for the next journey.

Clevercloggs pulled suitable garments from his rucksack.

Tizzie and the rest of the *Questers* went through the Traveller's Tunnel once more.

Everyone was soon ready to go.

'On this island there are great big Sacred Statues called, *Moai*,' said Mr Sand. 'Do not touch the Moai. They represent the ancestors of the Rapanui people who live there and they'll be very upset if you touch their ancestors.'

With this warning ringing in their ears, the *Questers* then linked arms to go back through the Crystal Door.

Clevercloggs led the way, putting his hand on the green crystal before saying their destination.

'Moai Beach, Iun Apar, Islandland, Ainaeco.'

FIFTY-ONE

Cyco The Sumo Cyclops

When Louis was next training in the arena, another Chewing Creature was there... Cyco the Sumo Cyclops.

Louis knew from the Programme of Dread that Lieutenant Liskeard was due to fight the Cyclops in the Colosseum.

To Louis, Cyco looked a bit like a giant Japanese sumo wrestler.

But he obviously wasn't purely human.

He must be a mutant, thought the young boy.

There was a single, huge, slanted eye on Cyco's forehead.

Louis was fascinated by the eye.

He wanted to know more about the strange looking creature.

Listening to some of the others talking, Louis learned that Cyco was created on one of the Napaj Islands in Far East Aisa.

He was a psychedelic Cyclops.

This meant his skin was all different colours, the result of pigmentation experiments by the mutationeers of Napaj.

His head was blue, his arms were green, his body was yellow, and his legs were red.

To Louis, it looked like lots of different buckets of fluorescent paint had been thrown at him.

Plumper said he'd heard the Cyclops had to eat things of all different colours to stay healthy, but Louis wasn't at all sure that this could be true.

Although he only had one eye, the Cyclops had *two* mouths.

He had a little mouth on his blue face.

And a huge mouth on his yellow belly.

He only used the face mouth for talking and drinking.

He ate with the belly mouth.

Having two mouths meant he could talk and eat at the same time.

During a rest period, Rudarius went off to check on something.

Whilst the trainer was gone, Louis just couldn't resist trying to get a closer look at Cyco's great big slanted eye.

He began walking towards the centre of the arena.

'I don't think you should get too near it, Prince Louis,' said Plumper, as he stood up to try to pull his friend back.

'It's all right,' said Louis.

'Look, he's chained to that post by his leg.'

Plumper tried to be firmer with Louis.

'No, Cyco is very dangerou...'

'Let him go,' said the guard, who had a wicked grin on his face as he pushed Plumper to the ground.

'You go on over there and have a good close look, lad.'

The guard's grin got bigger and bigger as Louis slowly made his way nearer and nearer towards Cyco the Sumo Cyclops.

FIFTY-TWO

Queen Avareipua Of The Rapanui

The *Questers* arrived on the island of Iun Apar on a beautiful beach.

Looking up at the cliffs, Tizzie couldn't believe her eyes. Mr Sand had spoken of big statues, but those she could see at the top were absolutely huge.

The *Questers* climbed a winding cliff path.

The map was blinking to show them that they would find the Indigo Crystal very near the statues.

Once they had made their way to the top of the cliff, they were greeted by a group of heavily tattooed Rapanui warriors, all carrying spears tipped with razor-sharp obsidian.

Luckily, some of the warriors knew Clevercloggs well, and he was welcomed with open arms.

The *Questers* were taken to meet Queen Avareipua, the leader of the Rapanui.

The Queen listened carefully as Clevercloggs explained all about their quest to find the stones of the *Amulet of Hope* and the plan for the uprising against Emperor Evile.

When the wise old gnome had finished, the Queen spoke.

'I know of the gem stone you seek. Godolphin the Great visited our ancestors and left the stone here.

'It is one of the eyes of Paro, our tallest statue, but we don't know which one.'

FIFTY-THREE

I Spy

'Louis walked towards the centre of the arena and had very soon moved into Cyco's wide field of vision.

The Chewing Creature stared at the boy with his great big slanted eye.

He was shovelling great handfuls of food into his big belly mouth.

'I Cyco, I Cyco, I Cyco.'

The Cyclops repeated his name three times whilst continuing to feed as Louis got closer.

Louis was fascinated by the fact that Cyco could talk with his face mouth whilst at the same time eating with his belly mouth.

'Hi Cyco,' said the young boy, 'I'm Louis.'

'We play game of *I Spy?*' asked Cyco, as if he wanted to be friends.

'Okay,' said Louis innocently.

Both of Cyco's mouths seemed to grin at the same time as he began the game.

'I spy, with my BIG EYE, something beginning with '*F*'!'

'Fence?' guessed Louis, looking around him.

'No.'

'Fly?'

'No.'

'Don't know,' said Louis, 'I give up.'

'Come, and I tell answer,' said Cyco, beckoning Louis forward with a waggle of one of his huge thick fingers.

'Noh...' Plumper's warning was stifled by the guard's hand over his mouth.

Louis stepped forward.

'FOOOOOD!!!!'

Cyco made a clumsy lunge for Louis as he screamed the answer at the top of his voice.

Completely startled by Cyco's change of mood, Louis just managed to duck under the outstretched arms of the Cyclops and roll away.

Cyco took step after step as Louis rolled and rolled away as fast as he could.

Tggg.

Luckily, after five steps, Cyco couldn't keep chasing Louis because the restraining chain around his ankle tugged his leg and would allow him no more slack.

'Phew!' sighed Louis with relief, as he rose to his feet, dusted himself off and made his way back to Plumper.

The little gnome was shaking his head and wagging his finger.

'Hahaha!'

The guard was laughing heartily.

'That'll teach you to get too near a Chewing Creature, lad.

'You nearly became part of his lunch... Hahaha!'

Louis felt a bit silly that he had been so trusting and decided he wouldn't be getting close to any more Chewing Creatures if he could possibly help it.

FIFTY-FOUR

The Eyes Of Paro

The *Questers*, Queen Avareipua, and her Warrior Guards, made their way along the short path back to Moai Beach.

They stopped in front of the row of giant Moai statues.

Tizzie counted the statues.

Fifteen.

They were all standing on a stone platform which Mr Sand said was called an *ahu*.

The Moai faced in towards the land.

Their heads seemed much too big for their bodies.

They all had painted eyes except the tallest one, Paro.

He had two indigo jewels for his eyes, which sparkled as they reflected the sunlight.

'The ancestors face the land with their backs to the sea,' said the Queen. 'They watch over our territory to protect us.

'Only our people should touch the Moai, so I will instruct a warrior to climb up and get the crystal. But which eye do you wa... ?'

Just as the Queen was finishing her sentence, an indigo laser beam shot from the right eye of Paro and hit Jack's body, right over his heart.

'Ohhhhhh!'

There were gasps from the Rapanui as they stared in wonderment at the laser beam shining from Paro's eye.

FIFTY-FIVE

The Sixth Rainbow Crystal: Indigo

'Thank you, Your Highness, but our wizard should be able to retrieve the stone,' said Clevercloggs as the indigo laser continued to shine on Jack's heart.

All eyes were now on Jack as he pointed his wand and said, 'indigo stone come here', in Kernewek.

'*Men eyndygo omma dos.*'

The stone wiggled about in its socket before falling out towards the ground.

'Ohhhhhh!'

There were more gasps from the Rapanui as Jack quickly stepped forward a couple of paces and caught the Sixth Rainbow Crystal in his open palm.

The *Questers* thanked Queen Avareipua and said their goodbyes.

She promised that the warriors of Ainaeco would be ready when the time came for the uprising.

Once the *Questers* had all lined up with their hands on each other's shoulders as before, Clevercloggs bent down, put the crystal end of the Golden Key on the ground, and said the words Tizzie now knew so well: '*Golden Cavern, by the power of Godolphin.*'

'OHHHHHH!'

There were even louder gasps from the Rapanui people as the *Questers* disappeared into the ground.

FIFTY-SIX

Child Gladiators

At his next training session, Louis noticed lots of other children of various ages there, some even younger than him.

He soon learned the reason why from Plumper.

'They're the children that have been badly behaved at school. It's all down to Miss Wendron, the new Regulator of Schools in Wonrekland.

'One of her first regulations was that, for three cases of bad behaviour in school, naughty children would be imprisoned and sold into slavery.

'But when she heard that King Manaccan wanted as many fighters as possible for the Gladiator Games, Wendron had an idea.

'The wrinkled old hag suggested that, of every two children imprisoned, one would be sold into slavery as in the original plan; but the others would be sent to the Colosseum... to fight in the arena. The new King thought that was a great idea.'

So now Louis knew why there were dozens of children training as Child Gladiators.

He felt very sorry for them.

And as he watched them practising with their little swords and shields, another thought came into his head...

I'm so glad I don't go to school here in Erthwurld.

FIFTY-SEVEN

The Irupahtrit Springs

Back in the Golden Cavern, the *Questers* looked at the Godolphin Map for their next destination.

Jack pointed his wand.

'*Golow an mappa.*'

A violet light began blinking on the map.

Princess Kea said the location: 'The Irupahtrit Springs in Tebit.'

'Plateauland,' mused Mr Sand, deep in thought. 'Also known as, *the roof of the wurld.* It's the highest region on Erth.'

'Very remote and hard to get to.'

'Unless, of course, you've got a Crystal Door!' said Clevercloggs, beaming.

'Mount Kailash, where the springs are, is called the *Snow Jewel*, because it's always covered in snow and ice and the sunlight makes it glisten like a jewel.

'I'd say it's another great hiding place for a crystal of the *Amulet.*'

'Very much so,' agreed Mr Sand. 'Looks like we'll be needing warm clothes again.'

Clevercloggs used his rucksack, and the rest of the *Questers* went through the Traveller's Tunnel. Soon everyone had suitable warm clothes to go to Plateauland.

The magical rucksack and tunnel had also given them something else they would need.

Strange masks.

Tizzie held her mask to her face and asked: 'What's it for?'
Mr Sand answered.

'Since Plateauland is very high above sea level, there's a lot less oxygen in the air.

'For people who haven't grown up there, it can be very hard to breathe and there's a danger of getting dizzy and fainting.

'So make sure you use your mask as soon as you start feeling out of breath.'

The *Questers* then linked arms to go back through the Crystal Door.

Clevercloggs again led the way, putting his hand on the green crystal before saying their destination.

'Irupahtrit Springs, Tebit, Plateauland, Aisa.'

FIFTY-EIGHT

The Pool Of Jewels

The *Questers* arrived in Tebit at the base of a huge mountain.
Tizzie looked around.

A few hundred paces away, the awestruck young girl could see a
great many pools, each with a pillar of steam rising from its surface.

'The Irupahtrit Springs,' said Clevercloggs with an appreciative
smile. 'It's a long time since I've been here.'

The violet point of light on the Godolphin Map shined ever
more brightly as they approached the steaming pools.

Tizzie was already out of breath and feeling faint. She had
just put her breathing mask to her face when she saw a group of
riders approaching them.

Rather surprisingly, since he had been instantly recognised
everywhere else on their quest, none of the riders knew
Clevercloggs. They had, however, heard all about his adventures
and discoveries and asked him to prove his identity.

'Your leader is King Songtsan Gampo,' said Clevercloggs. 'I
came to his coronation. Must have been sixty years ago. He was
only thirteen at the time. Has a mole on his left cheek.'

The riders were sufficiently intrigued by the reputation of the
diminutive stranger in their land and his description of their king
that they took Clevercloggs and the other *Questers* to see their
leader.

When they arrived at the Tebitan camp, the King, who was
about seventy years old as far as Tizzie could make out, spoke first.

'Why, if it isn't Clevercloggs the Explorer!

'Hello, old friend.'

The King then listened intently as Clevercloggs explained all about their quest to find the Crystals of the *Amulet of Hope* and the plan for the rebel uprising against Emperor Evile.

When the wise old gnome had finished, the King spoke again.

'The gem stone you seek is in the Pool of Jewels. Godolphin the Great visited our ancestors and left it here. But the Great Wizard put hundreds of violet crystals in the pool. And, as you'll see, he made it very difficult to identify and retrieve the real one. How will you know which is the stone of the *Amulet* and how will you be able to remove it from the Pool of Jewels?'

'Because we have brought our very own Rainbow Wizard,' said Clevercloggs, with a smile and a nod in Jack's direction.

'But he's just a boy,' said King Songtsan Gampo, with a frown and a derisory shake of his head.

'Yes,' countered Cleverclogs with a grin, 'he's exactly the same age as a young man I saw crowned a king a long time ago in this very place. That person certainly proved worthy of the responsibility placed on his shoulders. So perhaps this other young man should be given the chance to do the same.'

'Fair comment,' smiled the King, nodding his head as he did so.

'I'll take you to the pool.'

FIFTY-NINE

The Crystal Illusion

The *Questers* followed King Songtsan Gampo to the Pool of Jewels.

Tizzie stared down into the tiny shallow pool. It was hard to see because of the hot steam rising from the water, but she could just make out lots of violet gems below the surface. There were so many that they covered the entire bottom of the pool.

'Haven't people tried to steal the stones?' asked Princess Kea.

'Well, I'm afraid that, for those who pass by, whether travellers or locals, the temptation is too great and they have indeed tried to steal them,' answered the King. 'But Godolphin had obviously thought of this. Put your hand in the water and try to take one.'

Remembering what had happened to Mr Sand and others who had tried to touch the other Rainbow Crystals, Princess Kea was now a little unsure whether she should have said anything. But she couldn't back down now.

She crouched down and stretched out her hand towards the hot pool. As she put her hand in and tried to pick up a couple of the crystals just below the surface, a strange thing happened. Her fingers just went straight through the stones, as if they weren't really there.

'They can't be picked up!' said Kea.

'Precisely,' said the King.

It was time for Jack to step forward.

SIXTY

The Seventh Rainbow Crystal: Violet

A violet laser beam shot from the pool and shined on the young wizard's heart as soon as he drew close to the Pool of Jewels.

He pointed his wand and said, 'violet stone come here', in Kernewek:

'*Men melyonen omma dos.*'

One of the violet stones immediately rose vertically out of the pool.

Tizzie watched it ascend until it was directly above their heads.

It hovered for a few moments as if deciding what to do next, and then descended slowly into Jack's open palm.

'At last, we now have all seven Rainbow Crystals,' said Mr Sand with a beaming smile.

The *Questers* thanked King Songtsan Gampo and said their goodbyes.

He promised that he would do all he could to make sure the warriors of Aisa were ready when the time for the uprising came.

The *Questers* all lined up with their hands on each other's shoulders.

Clevercloggs bent down and put the crystal end of the Golden Key on the ground.

'*Golden Cavern, by the power of Godolphin.*'

Tizzie and the other *Questers* disappeared into the ground.

SIXTY-ONE

Finding *Photos*

Back in the Golden Cavern, the *Questers* looked at the Godolphin Map for their next destination.

Jack pointed his wand.

'*Golow an mappa.*'

Nothing happened.

'*Golow an mappa.*'

Nothing again.

Tizzie wondered what could be wrong.

'Are you thinking what I'm thinking?' asked Mr Sand, looking at Clevercloggs as he spoke.

'Probably,' said the wise old gnome.

'What's the problem?' asked Princess Kea.

'Well, it looks as if we'll now need Godolphin's White Wand to discover the location of *Photos* using the map,' answered Clevercloggs.

'I thought that might be the case, which is one of the reasons I asked Pemberley and the other members of RAE in the castle to retrieve the White Wand and the *Amulet* from Godolphin's Chamber.

'Once they have the Wand and *Amulet*, they're going to hide them in a safe place away from the castle so that I can collect them.

'I was hoping to give them more of a chance to retrieve the items and hide them in my secret hiding place. That's why we've been going around Erthwurld collecting the *Rainbow Crystals* first.

'But, since it seems we need the White Wand before we can find and recover *Photos*, I've now got little choice.

'I *have* to take a chance and go to the hiding place and hope our friends have been able to carry out their task.'

Tizzie thought that the wise old gnome was really very clever and very brave as he stepped forward, put his hand on the Crystal Door, and said his destination.

As the green crystal softened, Clevercloggs stepped into the door once more.

SIXTY-TWO

Pemberley's Task

After receiving instructions from Clevercloggs, Pemberley had consulted Mrs Portwrinkle over the best way in which to perform the task successfully.

The brave butler had been gathering intelligence, by watching all the goings-on at the castle using his secret network of corridors and peepholes.

Meanwhile, Mrs Portwrinkle had spoken to Bartholomew Bude, the castle gardener.

The plans had been made.

Today was the day.

Pemberley was watching through the peephole that gave him a view of Godolphin's Chamber.

He had a clear view of the glass cabinet that contained the White Wizard's Wand and the *Amulet of Hope*.

The chamber was guarded all the time, day and night. A good thing was that the guards were *outside* the door most of the time.

Since there was only one door and no windows, he presumed that nobody expected an intruder to simply emerge *inside* the room.

However, he did have a worrying concern: the guards checked inside the room a few times every hour.

Although the checks were not that frequent, Pemberley's problem was that he had not been able to ascertain any pattern to them. They appeared to be completely random.

That meant he had no way of knowing precisely *when* a guard would enter the room.

If he was caught with his hand in the cabinet, his cover would be blown and he would be executed, or, perhaps worse, sent to the Colosseum.

It was also possible that other members of RAE would be exposed.

That would be a very bad thing.

He and Mrs Portwrinkle had therefore devised a plan that would ensure the guards were occupied whilst Pemberley was inside Godolphin's Chamber retrieving the White Wand and the *Amulet*.

They had decided to repeat the use of a weapon that had worked very well before...

Mrs Portwrinkle's Pastys.

SIXTY-THREE

Creaking Doors, Floors, and Cabinets

Pemberley heard Mrs Portwrinkle outside the door.

'Here we are then, one lovely pasty each.'

As expected, he then heard the guards' appreciation.

'Great, Mrs Portwrinkle, thanks.' 'Marvellous.'

Mrs Portwrinkle then engaged the guards in conversation as planned. When a good chat was underway, the trembling butler seized his chance. He tentatively opened the secret doorway from his peeping passageway and stepped into Godolphin's Chamber.

Crrkkk. The door creaked. Far too loudly for his liking. He made a mental note to make sure he oiled the hinges in future.

Now the brave butler tiptoed across the room.

Crrkkk. Now the floor was creaking too!

Still the guards didn't hear. Mrs Portwrinkle was certainly keeping them occupied. He wasn't that surprised. After all, small-talk and gossip were two things she was really expert at.

Moments later, Pemberley was at the cabinet. He opened the door, warily. Crrkkk. Another creak! Luckily, Mrs Portwrinkle was *still* talking. The butler felt his heart pumping as he put his hand in and retrieved the White Wand and the *Amulet*. He quickly put them in his inside jacket pocket.

From another pocket, he produced a replica of each item.

After putting back the replicas in exactly the same positions as the originals, Pemberley quietly left the room the same way he came in. Nobody would have known he'd been there.

SIXTY-FOUR

'Did You Get Them?'

Pemberley emerged through one of his secret doors into the corridor that led to the kitchen of the castle.

He arrived in the kitchen just before Mrs Portwrinkle, who bustled in a few moments later with a tray containing two empty plates.

The guards had obviously enjoyed their pastys.

There were lots of other people in the kitchen, all preparing food according to Mrs Portwrinkle's instructions.

The chief cook looked enquiringly at the butler across the kitchen, as if to ask, 'did you get them?'

He nodded in the affirmative and moved his head and eyes towards the pantry door, as if they should meet in there.

In the pantry, behind the closed door, Pemberley handed the White Wand and the *Amulet* to Mrs Portwrinkle, who quickly wrapped them in a cloth and secreted them somewhere beneath her voluminous petticoats.

Satisfied that they would be quite safe there, Pemberley left the pantry with a whole cheese on a wooden board, in order to justify his presence in the kitchen in case there were any of Manaccan's spies amongst the staff.

Moments later, Mrs Portwrinkle was heading for the castle gate.

SIXTY-FIVE

Brave Mr Bude

Bartholomew Bude was driving his horse and cart towards the castle gate.

Mrs Portwrinkle walked straight towards the old gardener and handed him a small bag saying, in her loudest voice...

'There you are Bart, a little snack for you on your trip today.'

There were lots of guards around but this overt activity was less likely to arouse suspicion than if she had tried to hand the bag over more surreptitiously.

The gregarious cook was regularly to be seen handing out special food treats to all sorts of people around the castle.

'Why thank you, Mrs Portwrinkle,' said Bude, equally theatrically. 'That'll keep me going all day.'

With that, Mrs Portwrinkle hurried away.

Bartholomew Bude now had to get past the guards at the gate.

They were under instructions to thoroughly search everybody who came in or out of the castle.

When he got to the gate, the old soldier was trembling inside. But he didn't let it show.

To outward appearances, he was as cool as one of his prize cucumbers.

The guards searched Mr Bude and his cart but, having seen Mrs Portwrinkle hand over his packed lunch in full view of everyone, they didn't seem to feel it necessary to search the little bag.

The guards let him proceed.

Phew!

Once on the other side of the gate, Bart sighed with relief.

He had made it out of the castle with the bag.

Now he just needed to get to his destination and put it in the special hiding place.

He hoped he would be in time for Clevercloggs to collect it.

SIXTY-SIX

There Was Nobody There

Clevercloggs arrived at Washaway Wood in the Playing Place, next to the pond.

The little village of higgledy-piggledy houses was empty.

There was nobody there.

All the other gnomes were in the dungeons.

Clevercloggs already knew this and was expecting it to be deserted.

But the ghostly quiet of his home still saddened him greatly.

The wise old gnome made his way over to the sandpit.

He searched and searched amongst the grains of sand, but the package he was looking for was nowhere to be found.

As he had thought, Pemberley and the others had not had time to get the White Wand and the *Amulet*.

For once, Clevercloggs was unsure what to do next. Should he wait and risk being seen? That was very dangerous. There was a reward for the capture of gnomes all over Wonrekland, and he was wanted for murder. Should he go? But then he'd only have to come here again to find out if the others had been successful in retrieving the Wand and the *Amulet*.

Then, just at that moment, he heard one of the best sounds in the wurld coming from over the hill on the road into Washaway Wood.

'Whstllll. Whstlllll. Whstllll.'

He'd know that wonderful mellow whistle anywhere.

It was Bartholomew Bude!

SIXTY-SEVEN

The *Amulet Of Hope*

Clevercloggs arrived back in the Golden Cavern to the congratulations – and obvious relief – of his fellow *Questers*.

After the welcome, he reached into the little cloth bag that he'd collected from Bartholomew Bude.

Tizzie watched as the old gnome first held up the *Amulet of Hope*, saying, 'It's time to put the Rainbow Crystals back where they belong.'

Clevercloggs then laid the *Amulet* on a ledge protruding from the wall of the Golden Cavern.

The *Amulet* was made of copper.

It was about the size of a saucer and had a chain attached to it so that it could be worn around the wearer's neck.

Jack took the pouch in which he'd put all the Rainbow Crystals and, instructed by Clevercloggs, scattered its contents on the little ledge beside the *Amulet*.

'But there are no holes for the crystals, where do they fit?' asked Jack.

'You'll see,' said Clevercloggs. 'Just wait a moment.'

Tizzie wondered what would happen.

To her astonishment, the Rainbow Crystals began rolling towards the *Amulet* of their own volition; first the Red Crystal, then the Orange Crystal, and so on, until a line of seven little crystals had formed and was making its way slowly towards the *Amulet*.

The line of crystals hopped right on to the flat circle of copper, and rolled around it in turn.

The Rainbow Crystals only stopped moving when the last one was on board.

Tizzie noticed that the crystals had stopped at seven regular intervals around the circle.

Then she watched in awe as something even more amazing happened.

The crystals began to glow as they got hot.

Very hot.

There was a fizzing sound as the metal of the *Amulet* began to melt beneath each of the seven crystals as they got hotter and hotter.

The seven coloured gem stones began sinking into the copper.

Then, suddenly, the sinking stopped.

The Rainbow Crystals now appeared to be securely set in the *Amulet of Hope*.

'The *Crystal Ring*,' said Mr Sand, in a reverential tone, as if everyone knew what he was talking about. 'Now we just need *Photos* for the centre and the *Amulet* will be complete again.

'We'll leave it to cool for a few moments,' said Clevercloggs.

'Meanwhile, young man, I've got something else for you.'

All eyes were on Clevercloggs as he reached into the little cloth bag once more.

SIXTY-EIGHT

The White Wand

Clevercloggs pulled Godolphin's White Wand from the little cloth bag.

Now he stretched out his left hand with the palm open.

'Hand me your Red Wand.'

Jack placed his wand gently into the gnome's palm.

Clevercloggs now handed him Godolphin's White Wand.

'We will soon know if you are worthy of this wand.

'Are you ready to try?'

'I am,' said Jack, his voice quaking with nerves.

The *Questers* gathered around the Godolphin Map, hoping that their next destination would soon be revealed.

Jack pointed his new White Wand.

'*Golow an mappa.*'

Nothing happened.

Tizzie saw Mr Sand looking anxiously at Clevercloggs.

Jack was obviously letting his nerves get to him.

'Relax,' said Clevercloggs. 'Take three deep breaths; then try again.'

Jack breathed deeply three times... then pointed the White Wand and spoke much more confidently.

'*Golow an mappa.*'

This time, a bright white light began blinking on the map.

'*Photos*!' exclaimed Clevercloggs as Jack zoomed in on the map using his new wand. 'It's in Eporue, on the island of Eterc in Eceerg.'

'That would make a lot of sense,' said Mr Sand as he looked at the little white light blinking on the map.

'Yes,' agreed Clevercloggs, as if deep in thought.

Jack smiled with relief at Tizzie.

She smiled back.

'Great,' said Princess Kea. 'Well done, Jack.'

'Well done, indeed,' echoed Mr Sand, smiling broadly.

'Yes, it certainly seems as if the apprentice has grown into a Rainbow Wizard,' smiled Clevercloggs.

He then became more serious.

'We can only hope that he has acquired enough of the *Three Qualities* to produce the Bright Beam.'

With that, the little gnome used his rucksack whilst the rest of the *Questers* went through the Traveller's Tunnel and soon everyone had suitable garments for a journey to the hot island of Eterc.

The magical rucksack and tunnel had also given them something else they would need: long sticks, each with a lump of something on the end.

Tizzie held up her long stick with an inquisitive look on her face.

'What's this?'

SIXTY-NINE

Noiretsa The Minotaur

'It's a torch,' said Mr Sand.

'Why have we got them?' asked Jack.

'Not sure,' answered Clevercloggs. 'But I'd imagine it could have something to do with *The Labyrinth of Sossonk*.'

'Yes,' said Mr Sand. 'The island of Eterc is the home of one of the most fearsome creatures in Erthwurld... the man-eating Minotaur. It lives in an underground system of tunnels called *The Labyrinth of Sossonk*. If we have to go into the Labyrinth, we'll need these torches to light our way.'

Tizzie had heard about the Minotaur that lived in a Labryinth, but she thought it was just a story and she couldn't remember much, so she just listened as Clevercloggs explained more.

'Part man and part bull, the creature lives in a system of dark tunnels below the Palace of Sossonk.

'Although a labyrinth usually has only one route through to the centre, this one is more like a maze. In the tunnels, there are many routes and many dead-ends. Once you enter the Labyrinth, you can easily get lost and die of thirst or starvation.

'And then, of course, there's the added danger of meeting the Minotaur.

'His name is Noiretsa.

'He roams the tunnels, under instructions to kill anyone who enters them. He charges and spears intruders with his sharp horns and tramples them with his hooves. Then he eats them.'

'According to legend,' added Mr Sand, 'the Minotaur is guarding a secret. Now we know what that secret is.'

'*Photos*!' said Jack.

'Yes,' said Clevercloggs. 'And to get that Eighth Crystal for the *Amulet*, we need to get to the Centre of the Labyrinth without being speared, trampled, or perhaps even eaten by Noiretsa.'

'I'm glad we've each got one of these torches to light our way,' said Mr Sand. 'They'll help us find our way through the Labyrinth to collect *Photos*. The blobs at the end of each torch are made of sulphur and lime, which means they'll even stay lit if they're plunged in water. It's important that they're reliable, especially if we get separated underground. Your only chance of escaping the charge of the Minotaur is if you see him coming in time and if you can see where to run.'

Tizzie now began to worry even more.

She tried not to imagine what it would be like to get lost and separated from the others and meet Noiretsa the Minotaur in a dark, underground tunnel.

With this worry-thought in the front of her mind, Tizzie linked arms with the other *Questers* to go back through the Crystal Door once more.

Clevercloggs again led the way, putting his hand on the green crystal before saying their destination.

'Palace of Sossonk, Eterc, Eceerg, Eporue.'

SEVENTY

The Palace of Sossonk

The *Questers* arrived on the Island of Eterc a few hundred paces from a huge stone building.

'The Palace of Sossonk,' informed Clevercloggs. 'Home to King Minos.'

At the gate, Clevercloggs was greeted by the guards and was taken immediately to see the King.

'I've been expecting you,' said King Minos to Clevercloggs as the *Questers* arrived in the Throne Room.

'News travels fast around RAE!' said Clevercloggs.

'Yes indeed,' said the King.

'We've discovered what the Minotaur is guarding,' said Clevercloggs. 'It's *Photos*, the main stone of Godolphin's *Amulet of Hope*.'

'That is correct,' said the King.

'How did you know?' asked Clevercloggs.

'The Kings of Eterc have long been entrusted with the guardianship of *Photos*,' answered Minos. 'It has been a secret known only to each King and passed from father to son for hundreds of years.'

'Well I never,' said Mr Sand. 'A real honour.'

'Indeed,' said King Minos, 'but it has also been a heavy burden… keeping such an important secret for so long.'

'It seems you have all done your job well, Your Highness,' said Clevercloggs. 'Because nobody knew.'

'We have taken the task we were given very seriously,' said the King. 'Now it would seem that it has all been for a purpose. Assuming, of course, that you have the other Rainbow Crystals, to boost the power of *Photos* in any battle with *Skotos*?'

'We have all seven of them,' confirmed Clevercloggs.

'What about the copper *Amulet* itself?' asked the King. 'And Godolphin's White Wand?'

'Got them too,' smiled Clevercloggs.

'But have you a powerful Rainbow Wizard to wear the *Amulet* and wield the Wand?' queried the King. 'I heard the wizards were all killed in the Prism Chamber explosion, except for Violothan.'

'All but *two* Rainbow Wizards are gone,' said Clevercloggs. 'Violothan, as you know, has chosen the Path of Darkness. But there is one wizard left who may be able to do battle with him.'

As he spoke, the little gnome rolled his eyes in Jack's direction.

'An apprentice,' mused King Minos as he followed Clevercloggs' gaze.

Tizzie could see the King was looking at Jack very carefully – and, it has to be said, a little sceptically – as he asked the big question on his mind.

'Does he possess enough of the *Three Qualities* to enable him to produce the Bright Beam with Godolphin's Wand and the *Amulet*?'

Clevercloggs' answer did not exactly inspire Jack with confidence.

'We won't know that until we find *Photos*.'

SEVENTY-ONE

The Clew To The Labyrinth

King Minos led the *Questers* to the entrance of the Labyrinth. Tizzie stared at the huge wooden door. It was enormous.

The King had the key to the door on a cord around his neck. He opened the door.

'There are more than thirteen hundred cells of the Labyrinth. Without a guide, it is impossible to know which route to choose.'

From his pocket, he now produced a thin thread, tightly wound into a ball.

'Here, take this ball of thread. It's called a *clew*. Godolphin left it here. He said that the traveller who could rightfully collect *Photos* would be able to use the clew to find the Centre of the Labyrinth and retrieve the *Crystal of Light*; and then use the clew to find the way back out again.'

Clevercloggs took the clew and immediately handed it to Jack.

The *Questers* lit their torches, went through the door, and descended the steps into the dark Labyrinth.

Tizzie was last to go through the door.

She saw a tunnel straight ahead as she neared the bottom of the steps.

A shiver went up her spine as she put her foot on the hard stone floor of the tunnel.

SEVENTY-TWO

Using The Clew

As soon as Tizzie had reached the bottom of the steps, Jack spoke.

'Do you think I should attach one end of the clew to something, to let it unwind from here?'

'I think that would be a very good idea,' said Clevercloggs, smiling as if he was extremely pleased that Jack had thought of that on his own. Jack tied the loose end of the clew to a metal torch holder on the wall of the tunnel.

'You lead, Jack,' said Clevercloggs. 'After all, you have the clew, and I think, in your hands, it may guide us straight to the Centre of the Labyrinth. After a few more paces, they had to make a decision. They had come to a T-junction.

'Close your eyes and concentrate,' said Clevercloggs.

'Left or right? Ask inside for the answer.'

Jack closed his eyes. Tizzie couldn't bear the anticipation. What if her friend got it wrong?

'Left,' chose Jack. The *Questers* took the left turn.

But, after just two steps, the clew suddenly started to vibrate. However hard he tried, Jack could not unwind it any further. Now the thread started contracting, pulling Jack back towards the junction.

'I think the clew is telling you it's a right turn, young man!' said Mr Sand with a smile.

SEVENTY-THREE

Lair Of The Minotaur

Having taken the right turn at the junction, and with a lot more help from the magical clew, Jack led the *Questers* through the Labyrinth at an amazing pace.

Tizzie knew that, with every step, they were nearing the Centre, where their prize awaited: *Photos*, the *Crystal of Light*.

But the little girl knew something else.

The Centre was also the lair of the man-eating Minotaur... and 'man-eating' didn't mean that the beast would just eat men and boys... it would just as happily eat women... and *girls*.

'It appears that we will soon be there,' said Mr Sand, as he looked down at the strongly glowing point of white light on the Godolphin Map.

'Yes,' said Clevercloggs. 'That's good.

'But it also means we're getting close to Noiresta's lair.'

Mr Sand now spoke in a warning tone.

'Princess Tizzie, make sure you stay in the middle of the group.'

He then gave an instruction to the other *Questers*.

'Weapons ready.'

SEVENTY-FOUR

The Centre Of The Labyrinth

The *Questers* turned a corner and suddenly they were at the doorway of the *messi*, the central room of the Labyrinth.

'Shhhhhhh,' said Clevercloggs, putting his finger to his lips.

'Talk in whispers. We don't want to rouse Noiretsa.'

The doorway they were standing in was very high. Through it, Tizzie could see that the messi was small and square.

She followed Clevercloggs and Mr Sand into the room.

In the middle was a square slab of marble rock, about two paces long on each side and about the height of Tizzie's waist.

On top of the slab was a much smaller square of marble, about a foot long on each side.

On top of the smaller slab, set in a small hollow, was a tiny clear crystal, which glowed ever-so-slightly with a white light.

The steady glow would have been just enough to light the room if they didn't have their torches.

'So that little gem stone is the legendary *Photos*,' said Princess Kea.

'Good things often come in little packages,' smiled Clevercloggs. 'Hahaha!'

Everyone laughed a little.

But perhaps they had laughed too loudly.

Tizzie nearly jumped out of her skin as there was a death-defying roar behind them.

'MOAARRRRRRRRRRRRRRRRRRRR!'

SEVENTY-FIVE

Roar Of The Minotaur

'MOAARRRRRRRRRRRRRRRRRRRR!'

Tizzie quivered.

'MOAARRRRRRRRRRRRRRRRRRRR!'

She dropped her torch at the sight of the creature that was in the doorway. The beast had the body of a man but it was much larger than any human, and had much bigger muscles. The monster was covered in patches of fur.

Its head was that of a bull, with two huge horns sticking out at the sides.

'MOAARRRRRRRRRRRRRRRRRRRR!'

Stmmp!

The creature roared again and stomped its right leg, as if making ready to charge.

Princess Kea immediately raised her Kernowbow.

Mr Sand pointed his pistol.

'Hold your fire,' shouted Clevercloggs.

He then attempted to pacify the creature in-between its roars.

'MOAARRRRRRRRRRRRRRRRRRRR!'

Stmmp!

'Noiretsa, we are here to collect Godolphin's Crystal for the *Amulet of Hope*. We have brought with us a wizard who can touch the stone.'

As if to prove his point, a white beam of light suddenly shot from the little clear crystal and hit Jack in the heart.

This time, his whole body lit up with a bright light.

Wow! thought Tizzie as Jack glowed from head to toe.

'Moarrrrrrrrrrrrrrrrrrrr.'

This seemed to be enough to quiet the beast.

The huge Minotaur stood in the doorway, as if unsure what to do next.

SEVENTY-SIX

The White Crystal: *Photos*

Clevercloggs spoke in an urgent whisper.

'Jack, retrieve the stone. We must show the Minotaur you are the rightful collector.'

Jack pointed his White Wand at *Photos* and said in a trembling voice:

'*Men... gwynn... omma... dos.*'

Photos didn't move.

'Say it with confidence,' urged Clevercloggs.

'Like a man.'

Another voice now came out of Jack's mouth.

Not a boy's high-pitched voice.

But the stronger, deeper voice of a man.

'*MEN GWYNN OMMA DOS.*'

At that very instant, there was an explosion of bright white light from the tiny crystal.

The whole room lit up in a blinding flash.

As everyone regained their sight after the flash, all eyes were drawn to Jack.

There, resting in his open palm, was *Photos*, the *Crystal of Light*.

SEVENTY-SEVEN

A Task Completed

Nobody had seen the crystal move through the air.

It was as if it had been teleported directly into his hand.

Clevercloggs spoke again to the Minotaur.

'You can rest at last, Noiretsa. You have faithfully guarded the glowing stone, just as Godolphin asked you to.

'But now the rightful collector has come to take it back to where it belongs. Your task is completed.'

'Moarrr.'

Noiretsa sighed, as if a great, centuries-old, burden had suddenly been lifted. He gave what Tizzie thought was the slightest nodding smile, turned about, and left the doorway.

'Let's get back to the Golden Cavern,' said Mr Sand. 'We have important work to do.'

The *Questers* quickly got in line. Clevercloggs bent down and put the crystal end of the Golden Key on the ground.

'*Golden Cavern, by the power of Godolphin.*'

Back in the Golden Cavern, Clevercloggs placed *Photos* on the *Amulet* in the centre of the *Crystal Ring*. *Photos* glowed and sank into the copper as Clevercloggs spoke in an urgent tone.

'We have completed an important part of our task. We have Godolphin's White Wand and we have restored the Seven Rainbow Crystals and *Photos* to his *Amulet*.

'Now we must carry out the plan to begin the uprising and, of course, we must rescue Prince Louis.'

SEVENTY-EIGHT

Foreign Food

It was Louis' worst nightmare come true… foreign food.

Tonight was the night.

It was the eve of the Gladiator Games and there was going to be something called a 'Banquet of the Wurld'.

It was always a big affair apparently; a buffet of foods from all over Erthwurld.

For many of the contestants, this would be their last meal, and they were granted this one final luxury before they went to their deaths in the Colosseum.

The menu had been sent down in advance for the gladiators to see before the banquet.

Louis looked at the front page of the menu with dread.

There were pages and pages of horrible-sounding foods like deep-fried marmosets, pickled snails in their shells, jellied eels, poached aye-aye eyes, deep fried frog's legs, pig's trotters in garlic sauce, snake sausages, and guinea pigs on sticks.

Needless to say, when it came to the actual meal, Louis went hungry.

He just ate a bit of dry bread.

In contrast to the gladiators, the carniverous beasts and Chewing Creatures due to fight in the Colosseum had not been fed for days.

The plan was to make them as hungry as possible for the Games.

SEVENTY-NINE

Invisible Tizzie

The *Questers* were rehearsing the plan of what they were going to do.

The Gladiator Games would mark the beginning of the uprising against Evile.

A major part of the plan involved finding a way to rescue Louis, *before* he faced Og in the arena.

To her surprise, bearing in mind she was only ten, Tizzie was asked to play an important part in the plan.

Clevercloggs handed her a small vial containing a thick, dark blue elixir.

'One drop of this liquid will make you invisible for one minute. There are only twenty drops in the vial, so, if you drink it all before you begin your task, you will only have twenty minutes to complete it.'

He then went on to explain to Tizzie what they wanted her to do.

After he had finished explaining, the wise old gnome said: 'If you don't think you can manage that, please say so now. We wouldn't want you to do anything you don't feel able to do.'

Tizzie was not at all sure that she would be able to carry out the task.

But she knew how vital it was to the plan.

'I'll do my best,' she said bravely.

EIGHTY

The Gladiator Games Begin

The Gladiator Games began with the opening of the many entrances to the Colosseum.

As the huge queues of people – who were visiting from all over the Empire – streamed in and took their seats, there were warm-up entertainments to get people in the mood for the contests to come.

A succession of jugglers, tumblers, and jesters performed amazing and amusing acts for the crowd whilst the stadium filled up.

A large group of musicians played their instruments.

There were long straight trumpets called *tubicens*. One man played a large curved horn called a *lituus*. Another played a water-organ called an *organum*.

Professor Mullion had been forced to set up the eelectric sound system for the Colosseum, and the music boomed out from big speakers spread all around the stadium.

Although the large number of entrances meant that the stadium seats were filled as quickly as possible, there were twenty thousand spaces, so it took quite a while.

Finally, the stadium was full.

The noise from the excited crowd was deafening.

But the sound system was working well.

And this meant that the Master of Ceremonies could make announcements into his microphone that everyone could hear.

EIGHTY-ONE

The Colosseum Crowd

There were two types of people in the Conquest Colosseum crowd.

First, there were the good people of Wonrekland, who could be called, the 'home' supporters.

Most ordinary people in Wonrekland didn't want anything to do with the Gladiator Games as the Games were seen as a symbol of the Invader.

But these good people had been made to come and watch to ensure a good turnout for the Emperor.

Manaccan had threatened to take their children into slavery if they did not attend.

They had been told that Scurvy's spies would be on the terraces, watching for those who didn't cheer and wave at the right times.

The other section of the crowd was made up of the bad people.

They included the cronies in Evile's entourage whom Louis had watched coming over the bridge, as well as all the people who had come in with the eight warlords after the invasion.

These bad people could be called the 'away' supporters.

The new young King of Wonrekland was so confident that his new regime of Terror would maintain control that he hadn't separated the home and away supporters.

He had simply let everyone sit in any seat they wanted.

EIGHTY-TWO

The Imperial Box

King Manaccan sat waiting in the Imperial Box, which was situated amongst the middle front few rows on one side of the arena, so that the Emperor and his important guests had the best view.

Manaccan was surrounded by kings, chiefs, nobles, and warlords from all over Erthwurld.

But these were *his* Games.

And that meant a lot to him.

He felt like a very important person indeed.

Manaccan surveyed the capacity crowd in the Colosseum.

Good, he thought, the Emperor will be very pleased.

The new King of Wonrekland wanted to be satisfied that everything was ready.

He reviewed everything in his head.

Thousands of carnivorous beasts, dozens of Chewing Creatures, and hundreds of the wurld's top gladiators had been brought to the Games to make them a real spectacle.

Manaccan tried to remember the names of all the beasts who would be taking part: aligatorbats, lionbears, lizardrats, raptorhogs, rhinophants, scorpionsnakes.

There were far too many to recall without a written list.

Then there were the Chewing Creatures that the crowd, and, of course, the Emperor, would love so much: Chomp, Cyco, Grawl, Grinder, Mawl, Mulch.

Again, far too many for him to remember.

And, of course, there were the hundreds of gladiators who would take part.

Some were professional fighters, brought in from around the Empire especially for the Conquest Colosseum Games.

Others were amateurs – like the teachers, rebels, and troublemakers – who had been arrested, imprisoned, and then given a bit of training for their appearance in the Colosseum.

Marvellous, thought Manaccan smugly…

…everything is ready for the Emperor.

EIGHTY-THREE

Questers In Disguise

There was a third type of person in the Conquest Colosseum crowd: *Questers* in disguise.

Tizzie and the others had all dressed up so that they wouldn't be recognised.

It wasn't actually that difficult to go unnoticed since many of the people in the crowd were dressed in their native costumes from around the Empire.

There was such a mix of people that it seemed that *everyone* was strangely dressed.

Clevercloggs, Mr Sand, Princess Kea, Jack, and Tizzie each entered through five different entrances.

They had reasoned that, if one of them were recognised and apprehended, the rest would still be free to carry out the plan.

Misty was safely in Clevercloggs' pocket, so that he'd be ready to help in case there were any injuries.

The *Questers* took their seats along with all the other people in the crowd.

EIGHTY-FOUR

The Arena Of Blood

Blissfully unaware of the plans of the *Questers*, Manaccan surveyed the sandy floor of the arena with great satisfaction.

He had given specific instructions that the layer of sand should be deep.

It would need to be... to absorb the blood of the forthcoming battles.

Manaccan was looking forward to the blood.

And there was going to be lots of it to look forward to.

There would be beasts versus beasts, beasts versus creatures, creatures versus creatures, prisoners versus beasts, gladiators versus creatures, gladiators versus gladiators.

And, at the end of the day, there would also be Manaccan's favourite bout on the Programme of Dread – the Emperor's Champion Gladiator, Og the Ogreman, versus that troublesome little nuisance, Prince Louis the Assassin Boy.

Beneath the arena floor was a network of passages that housed the beasts, creatures, gladiators, and prisoners.

Manaccan was especially pleased with the amount of trapdoors in the floor... double the normal number.

These hidden doors in the floor could be opened at any time, thus allowing one of the carnivorous beasts or Chewing Creatures held below to escape and surprise the fighters in the arena.

The crowd always loved the trapdoor surprises because they never knew who or what would emerge from the hole in the ground.

To amuse the Emperor, Manaccan had also decided he would offer Evile the chance to pick some men and women of the home supporters from the crowd.

During the intervals between normal bouts, those chosen at random would be thrown into the ring to fight each other or be mauled by the carnivorous beasts and Chewing Creatures.

He thought this would add some extra excitement to the proceedings.

As Manaccan sat back, well satisfied with his plans and the attendance figures, a messenger entered the box and whispered in his ear.

The King gave an instruction for the trumpets to be sounded.

TTTtttrr! TTTtttrr! TTTtttrr!
TTTtttrr! TTTtttrr! TTTtttrr!

A deathly hush descended upon the Conquest Colosseum as twenty thousand people immediately fell silent.

The anticipation was palpable.

Everyone knew who was coming.

EIGHTY-FIVE

HAIL EVILE!

'HAIL EVILE!'
'HAIL EVILE!'
'HAIL EVILE!'

The people in the away crowd rose to their feet, saluted their special salute, and hailed their leader dementedly as Evile the Exterminator entered the Imperial Box from behind some purple curtains.

He was followed closely by Insomnia the Ice Maiden... and Violothan the Dark Wizard.

'Hail Evile.'

The home crowd were less enthusiastic in their cheering but went through the motions for fear of being noticed by Scurvy's Scum and losing their children to slavery.

The Emperor stood for a while in his purple robes, fanning his hand imperiously as he lapped up the applause.

As usual, Evile was wearing the infamous Purple Mask, which covered his whole face, with only a few small holes in it for him to see, talk, and breathe.

Even though he drank the special elixir that had kept him alive for so long, Evile was now so old that he felt it wise to hide his ghastly appearance from the people.

Finally, after much more applause, the Emperor sat down next to Manaccan.

The crowd fell silent once more.

The Master of Ceremonies rose on his podium to speak, his voice boosted considerably by the new eelectric microphone and speakers around the stadium.

Everyone listened in awe of the new technology as the MC read from his piece of parchment.

'His Imperiousness, Evile the Exterminator, in association with His Majesticness, Manaccan the Merciless, is very proud to announce the opening of the Conquest Colosseum and the commencement of Wonrekland's First Gladiator Games.'

With that, the Emperor and the King rose to their feet and lapped up more applause.

The away crowd saluted and hailed once more.

'HAIL EVILE!'

'HAIL EVILE!'

'HAIL EVILE!'

EIGHTY-SIX

Combat Commences

Suddenly, just as the crowd had saluted and hailed for the third time, a large trapdoor opened in the floor of the arena.

'OHHHHHHHHHH!'

A gasp of excitement went around the Colosseum.
Then there was a second of silence, before...

'EEEEEOOOOAAAAHHHHH!'

A rhinophant emerged from the trapdoor.
It made a trumpeting sound that caused Tizzie's whole body to shudder and shake.
The terrifying beast had been raised on a lift beneath the Colosseum and it now charged out into the arena.

'YESSSSSSSSS!'

The crowd shouted their appreciation.
Then there was another moment of silence as they waited to see the rhinophant's opponent.
Another trapdoor opened.

'EEEEEOOOOAAAAHHHHH!'

A second rhinophant emerged from the trapdoor, trumpeting loudly as it charged out into the arena.

'YESSSSSSSSS!'

The crowd shouted even louder than before. They knew that a fight between two rhinophants promised to be a gruelling and bloody battle to the death.

Each rhinophant had a huge horn and two long sharp tusks which it used as attack weapons.

The horns and tusks had been fitted with sharp metal points and each mutant beast wore protective guards around its eyes.

'EEEEEOOOOAAAAHHHHH!'
'EEEEEOOOOAAAAHHHHH!'

To Tizzie it seemed like the whole ground shook in the arena as the two rhinophants charged each other.

CLSSHH! BSSHH!
CLSSHH! BSSHH!

They were soon clashing and bashing each other ferociously as the crowd cheered them on.

The two great beasts did battle for over a quarter-of-an hour, before one of them, its body battered and its flesh torn, fell to the sand in the Arena of Blood.

Tizzie was even more disgusted by what she saw next.

Rather than being spared, the winner then faced twenty horse-mounted fighters armed with bows and lances.

'YESSSSSSSSS!'
'KILL!' 'KILL!' 'KILL!'

The screaming crowd called for more blood as the horsemen encircled their prey.

The exhausted beast stood no chance.

Mercifully, it was soon all over.

After the event, the bodies of the rhinophants were dragged off by blood-slaves to be thrown in the carrion pit, where vulturerats would feast on their carcasses to dispose of them.

Then sand-slaves came in with huge buckets to cover all the blood with fresh sand.

They used rakes to mix it in and then brushes to smooth the new sand.

Tizzie watched all this with increasing despair.

She had closed her eyes as each of the defeated rhinophants fell.

It was horrible.

But then an even more horrible thought came into her troubled mind...

It would soon be Louis' turn to enter the Arena of Blood.

EIGHTY-SEVEN

Flaming Chariots

After many more Chewing Creatures and carnivorous beasts had fought each other, it was time for the Fire Chariots.

Six chariots came into the arena. Each had two wheels with razor-sharp blades protruding from its axles.

The six charioteers, called *Essedari*, were armed to the teeth in readiness for mortal combat.

All six chariots were ablaze. The Essedari had to dispose of their opponents quickly, or be consumed by their own flaming chariot.

The blazing chariots sped across the arena in all directions, their occupants firing off arrows and throwing spears as they went.

Soon there were only two charioteers remaining.

The two survivors chased each other around and around, with each charioteer trying to cut up the wheels of his opponent's chariot with the blades on his axle.

The spokes on a wheel of one chariot were soon shredded. It turned over and the unfortunate charioteer was trapped under it as it skidded and rolled to a halt, right in front of the Imperial Box.

As flames and smoke rose from both chariots, the victorious gladiator jumped down and ran towards the loser, unsheathing his short sword as he went.

He held his gladius aloft, to await the Emperor's decision.

The crowd roared its wishes.

'LIVE!' 'LIVE!' 'LIVE!'

Evile raised his arm, and held it out in front of him, with his fist clenched and his thumb extended horizontally.

The crowd fell silent, waiting for the Emperor's decision.

Would he turn it up… for life?

Or down… for death?

Tizzie watched through her fingers, hardly able to look.

Thankfully, Evile turned his thumb upwards.

'Live!'

'HORRRAYYYYY!'

The crowd roared its approval and clapped his decision enthusiastically before saluting once more.

'HAIL EVILE!'

'HAIL EVILE!'

'HAIL EVILE!'

Behind the Purple Mask, the Evil Emperor basked in the applause.

He was in his element.

He loved the Gladiator Games.

EIGHTY-EIGHT

Surprise Fighters

'Arghhhh!'

Suddenly, Tizzie saw a man from the crowd drop from the stands and into the arena.

Crnch.

He landed with a crunch on the sand.

'OHHHH!'

The crowd gasped in delighted surprise.

This was a man the Emperor didn't like.

He had been invited to the Colosseum as a guest… only to be thrown, when he least expected it, into the Arena of Blood.

'Arghhhh!'

Now Tizzie saw another man from the crowd drop from the stands and into the arena.

Crnch.

He too landed with a crunch on the sand.

'OHHHH!'

The crowd gasped again.

Evile didn't care that he hadn't told his host about this unexpected development.

After all, he was the Emperor of the whole wurld.

He could do what he pleased.

The Exterminator rose to his feet and theatrically threw a very short dagger down onto the sand.

Clnk.

It landed with a dull clunk in front of the Imperial Box.

The two men looked at each other for a split second.

Each immediately realised he would have to get to the weapon first.

'YESSSSSSSSS!'

'KILL!' 'KILL!' 'KILL!'

The crowd screamed its approval of this surprise development as both terrified men ran for the dagger.

The man who had been thrown in second got to the weapon first.

The other man tried to take it from him.

The man with the dagger knocked the other to the ground.

'DIE!' 'DIE!' 'DIE!'

The crowd were screaming for blood.

Evile gave his permission for the victor to do the crowd's bidding.

'YESSSSSSSSS!'

The crowd roared as Tizzie looked away.

EIGHTY-NINE

Gladiators

Now it was the turn of the professional gladiators to fight.

Tizzie watched the barbarous spectacle through her fingers as the fighting went on.

There were all sorts of contests between all sorts of gladiators. An array of weapons and equipment was used. There were swords, and daggers, and spears, and shields, and helmets, and whips, and stones, and clubs.

At intervals, the crowd booed, then cheered, then roared, then fell silent, as the Gladiator Games progressed.

Eventually, it was the time for the Noxii, the criminal gladiators, to fight.

Some of them would fight each other.

Some of them would fight professional gladiators.

Tizzie knew that Louis would be fighting Og, the Emperor's Champion… the biggest and best gladiator of them all.

She also knew that her brother was top of the bill.

Although this meant his would be the last fight of the games, Tizzie was well aware that Louis' turn in the Arena of Blood was fast approaching.

She had an important part to play in the plan for his rescue.

And Mr Sand had just signalled that she should play it now.

Breathing anxiously and shaking with fear, Tizzie left her seat and walked down one of the long corridors inside the Colosseum building.

NINETY

Tizzie To The Rescue

Tizzie made her way to the Ladies' toilets.

Once on her own in there, she drank the whole vial of liquid that Clevercloggs had given her.

'Urgghhh.'

It tasted horrible.

Then she looked in a mirror.

There was no reflection. She was completely invisible.

The magic potion had worked!

Although nobody could see her, Tizzie was still very nervous as she made her way towards the steps that the guards took when they went down to the cells beneath the Colosseum.

Once at the top of the stone steps, she descended until she came to a pair of iron gates.

They were open. The guards had no need to lock them whilst the Gladiator Games were in progress.

Tizzie crept along the corridor until she came to another pair of gates. Fortunately, the keys were on her side of the gates and she used them to enter.

Now she was in the corridor where the Noxii prisoners were kept. There were only two guards, just as Clevercloggs had predicted. They were sitting at a table playing cards.

As she walked past each of the cells, she was surprised to find that the cell opposite the one containing the gnomes – and a sweet little sausage dog – did *not* contain Louis.

She was sure Clevercloggs had said Louis would be in that cell... but it was empty. Although very worried about her brother, Tizzie knew she must carry out the rest of her task.

She fumbled for a little tablet in her pocket.

As she took out the tablet, she kept it wrapped in her closed fist as Clevercloggs had told her to.

This meant it would remain invisible, shrouded by her unseen hand.

She then crushed the tablet in her fingers and sprinkled the resulting powder over the heads of the two guards.

They both dropped off to sleep instantly.

Plumper and all the other prisoners watched in stunned silence as the ring of keys from the head guard's belt rose into the air and floated towards their cell.

Tizzie threw the keys into the cell.

Longlegs wasted no time in grabbing them up and opening the cell door.

'Over here!' shouted the other prisoners. 'Us too.'

Soon, Lieutenant Liskeard and all the loyal Kernish soldiers were free.

In turn, they freed Miss Prudent and all the teachers and everyone else whom Superintendent Scurvy had imprisoned without reason or fair trial.

Tizzie watched the prisoners being freed; all the while hoping that Louis would soon appear from inside one of the cells.

But the increasingly desperate little girl had no idea that the plans for her brother had been changed just a short while earlier... by none other than the Emperor himself.

NINETY-ONE

First To Fight

In the Imperial Box, a few minutes before Tizzie had arrived in the cells to free the prisoners, Wonrekland's new young king had been just about to give instructions for the Noxii criminal contests to begin when the Emperor had leaned sideways towards him to speak.

'Manaccann.'

'Yes, Your Imperiousness.'

'Ii WANTT somethingg.'

'Speak Master, and I will obey.'

The Emperor whispered in Manaccan's ear.

He wanted to change the programme.

He wanted Og to go first as he simply couldn't wait to see his champion fight.

That was his personality.

He wanted what he wanted. And he wanted it… NOW.

He didn't care that Louis' bout was supposed to be at the top of the bill, the last fight at the end of the Games.

Manaccan was somewhat surprised and disappointed.

He had planned a Grand Finale with Louis versus Og as the main attraction.

But he daren't defy his master.

The Emperor always got what the Emperor wanted.

So it was decided. Og's bout would be next.

Which meant Louis would be the first of the Noxii to fight.

NINETY-TWO

OG! OG! OG!

Following Evile's 'request', Manaccan summoned a servant and gave instructions for the changes to the programme to be passed on to the Master of Ceremonies.

Clp. Clp. Clp.

He then clapped his hands three times.

TTTtttrr! TTTtttrr! TTTtttrr!

The trumpets sounded again.

The chattering crowd fell silent once more.

Another hush descended around the Conquest Colosseum.

The MC made the announcement.

'Citizens of The Empire, I give you the Emperor's Champion...

'OG... THEEEEE... OGREMAAAAAAAN!'

'Yeeeeeeeeeeeeeeessssss!'

The away crowd cheered and stomped their feet.

'OG! OG! OG!'

STMP! STMP! STMP!

'OG! OG! OG!'

STMP! STMP! STMP!

Then they started chanting at the tops of their voices...

'WE WANT OG!'
'WE WANT OG!'
'WE WANT OG!'

Louis had been dragged out of his cell just a few moments before Tizzie had arrived to free him.

He had been marched upstairs and was now standing in the Tunnel of Terror, waiting to walk down it into the Arena of Blood.

He could see a small portion of the crowd as he looked down the tunnel.

There was an incredibly loud noise coming from the packed arena. It was petrifying.

Og was standing next to him.

He turned to Louis, held his Ironhammer across his chest and said, 'Og,' bowing a little as he did so.

Louis was unsure as to how he should respond, so he followed Og's lead. He held his sword across his chest and said, 'Louis,' bowing a little, just as Og had done.

The Ogreman then began striding down the tunnel. Louis started to go with him, but four guards stepped forward and blocked his path. It was clear the two gladiators were to make separate entrances.

Louis stood still, watching and listening as his opponent entered the arena. His legs began shaking uncontrollably as he realised the full magnitude of what was just about to happen.

That fearful word was repeating in his head once more.

'*Ironhammer… Ironhammer… Ironhammer.*'

NINETY-THREE

'Bringg Inn Thee Boyy'

'OG! OG! OG!'
STMP! STMP! STMP!
'OG! OG! OG!'
STMP! STMP! STMP!

There was another eruption of cheering and foot stomping as the Emperor's Champion entered the Conquest Colosseum from the Tunnel of Terror. The cheering and stomping continued as Og strode into the centre of the Colosseum.

He faced the Imperial Box to acknowledge his Emperor.

The Ogreman then bowed deeply as he put his Ironhammer across his chest and said, 'Og'.

'OG! OG! OG!'
STMP! STMP! STMP!
'OG! OG! OG!'
STMP! STMP! STMP!

There was even more cheering and foot stomping as the Emperor's Champion bowed in all directions for the crowd.

Evile stood and raised his arm.

The cheering and stomping stopped immediately.

'Bringg inn thee boyy.'

NINETY-FOUR

David And Goliath

As he began to make his way down the Tunnel of Terror, flanked by the four soldiers to make sure he didn't make a run for it, Louis could see some of the crowd through the tunnel entrance. They were waving their arms and he could hear the chanting and stomping getting louder and louder with every step.

'OG! OG! OG!'

STMP! STMP! STMP!

'OG! OG! OG!'

STMP! STMP! STMP!

A little tear of fear ran down Louis' cheek.

Suddenly, an old man hobbled into his path.

The man looked him straight in the eyes.

Although the old man was cleverly disguised with big bushy hair and a long straggly beard, Louis knew those eyes.

They belonged to Mr Sand!

The look in the familiar eyes warned Louis not to say anything. He stayed quiet.

'Please sirs,' said the old man to the soldiers, 'I have a gift here for my grandson. Would you deny a grandfather a last chance to say goodbye?'

The guards knew Louis was a Prince of Forestland. But they had no idea who his grandparents were. There were so many people visiting Wonrekland for the Gladiator Games that this could easily be true.

They didn't want to say no.

If he were a royal grandfather, they could be in real trouble if they refused him his wish.

'And may I give him this?' asked Mr Sand. 'It's his favourite toy.'

'I'm not sure,' said one guard. 'Don't know if that's allowed. It looks like a weapon.'

'Oh, don't be silly,' said the senior guard, 'what possible harm could the boy do with that little thing?'

Mr Sand smiled in mock gratitude and came close to Louis, whispering so that the guards couldn't hear.

'There's very little time. Here, take your Kernow Catapult. Pemberley couldn't get the ammo belt, so we'll have to improvise.

'I have to ask you a question. Don't speak just nod. Do you remember the story of David and Goliath?'

Louis had recently learned about this story at school.

He nodded once.

'Good, so you'll know what to do with this.'

With that, Mr Sand clasped Louis' hand and passed him a small, round pebble.

NINETY-FIVE

Louis And Og

'BOOOO! HSSSS! BOOO!'

As Louis entered the Arena of Blood from the Tunnel of Terror, it was very clear that the away crowd was supporting his opponent.

'BOOOO! HSSSS! BOOO!'

The home crowd booed and hissed at him as well. In a way he could understand this. After all, they still believed he had killed their beloved King and Queen.

Louis faced Og in the centre of the Conquest Colosseum.

They stood about thirty paces apart.

Og raised his Ironhammer and set his huge shield into his huge shoulder. Louis knew it was pointless but he too raised his little shield and held up his little sword.

'OG! OG! OG!'

STMP! STMP! STMP!

'OG! OG! OG!'

STMP! STMP! STMP!

The crowd cheered as Og took his first step forward. Louis knew he had very little time to act. He quickly dropped his sword and shield... and took out his catapult.

He loaded the smooth stone... aimed... and fired!

NINETY-SIX

The Thumb Of Dread

Og fell to the ground the instant the pebble hit him on the temple.

'OOHHH!'

The crowd gasped in shock as Louis grabbed up his gladius and raced over to his massive opponent.

He raised his sword above his head as the Emperor's Champion lay unconscious before him on the ground.

Louis knew from his training that the *Way of the Colosseum* was harsh and cruel: kill or be killed.

But he also knew that he had to wait for the Emperor's approval. So he lowered his weapon a little.

The Emperor put out his arm. On the end of his arm was his clenched fist with the thumb sticking out to the side. Louis was far too far away to see but on each finger was tattooed a capital letter. On the little finger was the letter 'E'. On the ring finger was the letter 'V'. An 'I' was on the middle finger. Then an 'L' was on the index finger. And, on the thumb, was another 'E'. All five tattoo-letters spelled out the Emperor's name:

E-V-I-L-E

The crowd murmured. After what seemed like an age, the Emperor now turned his hand so that the thumb pointed down.

Louis knew this 'thumbs down' was the sign for... *Death*.

He gripped hard on the handle of his sword and gulped a deep breath as he raised the blade high above his head once more.

NINETY-SEVEN

A Hush Descended

Louis looked down at Og.

'Ogogoggg...'

The Ogreman mumbled as he stirred.

He was regaining consciousness.

He opened his eyes.

The giant mutant warrior quickly realised his fate.

He looked up at Louis and gave the faintest of smiles.

It was as if he were resigned to death, and giving the young boy permission to strike the fatal blow.

Louis looked deep into the Ogreman's eyes.

They were full of the pain of being made to fight and maim and kill again and again and again over many years.

Og now closed his eyes once more... and waited for the welcome relief that death would bring.

Louis held the sword aloft.

HSSSHHHHH...

A hush descended like a blanket of silence over the Conquest Colosseum.

NINETY-EIGHT

'Destroyy Thee Boyy!'

Louis just couldn't do it.

He could not kill Og.

The young boy threw away the sword and shouted at the top of his voice.

'I *WON'T* KILL HIM…

'AND I *DIDN'T* KILL THE KING AND QUEEN!'

The home crowd seemed to suddenly realise that Louis was one of them.

That he stood for Good. And Right. And Truth.

And they certainly seemed to admire his courage in defying the Emperor.

'Louis! Louis! Louis!'

A small chant began around the Colosseum.

'LOUIS! LOUIS! LOUIS!'

It got louder and louder.

'LOUIS! LOUIS! LOUIS!'

Now even some of the away crowd joined in.

Up in the Imperial Box, Manaccan shifted uncomfortably in his seat. He knew he had to quickly make an example of Louis, to show who was in charge.

But the Emperor was way ahead of him.

He told Violothan to use the Dark Beam.

'Darkk Wizardd… doo yourr dutyy…

'Destroyy thee Boyy.'

142

NINETY-NINE

Og's Last Act

Following Evile's instructions, Violothan brought *Skotos* from his pocket with his left hand whilst at the same time aiming his Violet Wand at Louis with his right.

'Death by *Skotos*! Die, boy!' he cried.

The Dark Beam emanated from the wand.

Suddenly, Og was on his feet next to Louis, pushing the defenceless young boy aside as he unleashed his Ironhammer in the direction of Evile.

The Ogreman had chosen to sacrifice himself for the prince who had shown such compassion towards him.

The Dark Beam struck Og's huge frame, sucking the life light from him right in front of Louis' eyes.

Up in the Imperial Box, Insomnia deflected the Ironhammer so that it narrowly missed the Emperor.

As Og shrivelled and fell, Violothan aimed at Louis again.

ONE HUNDRED

'Now, Jack... NOW!'

Mr Sand had positioned himself next to the MC's podium.

He jumped onto the platform, grabbed the microphone and shouted into it as loud as he could.

'Now Jack... NOW!'

Jack jumped into the arena from the terrace and rolled forward into a standing position facing the Imperial Box.

He then threw off his long, dirty brown coat, revealing the Red Robe of a Rainbow Wizard.

He wore the glistening *Amulet of Hope* around his neck.

He held up the White Wand.

His whole body glowed with a brilliant white light.

He muttered a spell in his new deeper voice.

What happened next caused a huge gasp of astonishment from the crowd.

'OHHHHHHH!'

ONE HUNDRED & ONE

The Bright Beam

'The Bright Beam... 'The Bright Beam...' 'The Bright Beam...'

A ripple of recognition went around the arena as a thin beam of white light emanated from Jack's wand. It was about three feet long.

His wand was now like a sword with a blade made of dazzlingly bright light.

Violothan had been momentarily distracted by all these events. But Evile brought him back to his senses.

'*DESTROYY* HIMM!'

Obeying his master's instruction, the Violet Wizard aimed again.

But some members of the home crowd, now given confidence by the presence of Jack and the Bright Beam, surged towards the Dark Wizard. This distracted Violothan momentarily. For an important split second, he seemed unsure as to where he should aim: Louis, Jack, or crowd.

The Emperor was now beside himself with rage.

'KILLL THEMM ALLL!'

Violothan unleased the terrible power of the Dark Beam into the surging section of the crowd. It fanned out in a cone shape, indiscriminately destroying all in its path.

'Arghhh.' 'Urghhh. 'Arghhh.' 'Urghhh.'

Two dozen people shrivelled to dust in an instant.

This had the desired effect. It halted the surging crowd.

ONE HUNDRED & TWO

'To The Highest Good...'

Violothan now aimed straight at Jack.

'Death by *Skotos*! Die, apprentice!' he cried.

The Dark Beam emanated from the Dark Wizard's wand.

At the very same moment, with his whole form glowing brightly, Jack pointed his White Wand and shouted...

'To the highest good... in the name of Omni!'

'OHHHHHHHHH!'

The crowd held its collective breath as the Bright Beam shot from Jack's wand and met the Dark Beam halfway.

A ball of lightning formed and sparks flew off in every direction as the two beams battled for supremacy.

'HOOORRRRAYYYY!'

Suddenly, the home crowd erupted as the Dark Beam appeared to be retreating in the presence of the Bright Beam.

The laser of dazzling light from Jack's wand extended further and further until it touched Violothan's wand.

The Dark Wizard's wand arm immediately went limp and fell down by his side. His wand fell to the ground. He went to pick it up with his other hand. Jack aimed the Bright Beam again, this time striking his adversary in the left shoulder. Now Violothan had *two* limp arms and he dropped *Skotos*.

'Phew!' Jack sighed with relief.

But whilst concentrating on his battle with Violothan, he had not seen Insomnia carefully aiming her crossbow at his own heart.

ONE HUNDRED & THREE

Now Is Our Chance

Beneath the Colosseum, Lieutenant Liskeard took charge.

'Come on everyone.

'Now is our chance for freedom and to fight for Good and Right.'

The gallant young officer then led the way as the prisoners grabbed up weapons from the armoury and overpowered the guards.

They all raced up the stone steps, charged along the Tunnel of Terror… and burst into the Arena of Blood, shouting their rallying cry at the tops of their voices.

'Onen hag Oll!'

'Onen hag Oll!'

'Onen hag Oll!'

The home crowd responded with their own roar.

'Onen hag Oll!'

Still invisible, Tizzie had hurriedly followed the prisoners.

She now became visible again as she ran down the tunnel.

As she entered the arena, all she could think about was one thing.

Where was Louis?

ONE HUNDRED & FOUR

Insomnia Strikes

Clevercloggs, vigilant as ever, *did* see Insomnia aiming her crossbow at Jack.

Thinking quickly, he threw a Cleverstick through the air to try to put her off her aim.

The Cleverstick exploded in a ball of water, which meant Insomnia was frozen for just an instant before her natural defences restored her ice-system to balance.

His action had put her off her aim… but not quite enough.

The bolt from the crossbow flew through the air, heading straight for Jack's back.

'Jack!' Having just entered the Arena of Blood, Tizzie screamed as she saw Insomnia fire.

Jack spun around to face Tizzie as the bolt was almost upon him.

But as the bolt came within inches of her friend's body, it seemed to bounce off the Bright Light that surrounded him. It was as if the light were acting like a force field, protecting him from harm.

Jack winked at Tizzie and gave her a little wave.

Azzzzzzzzzzttt! Just at that moment, an arrow from the air struck one of Evile's Imperial Guards.

Rzzzzzzzzzzttt! In the same instant, a rifle shot hit another guard.

Everyone looked up.

Hundreds of arrows and shots now rained down on the Imperial Guards from the air.

ONE HUNDRED & FIVE

Rebellion In The Air

Tizzie looked up.

There were hundreds of eagleponies in the sky.

On their backs sat the Redskins and Settlers of Acirema North.

More carefully aimed arrows and shot balls hit Evile's soldiers as they scattered for cover. The Imperial Guards returned fire with bows, crossbows, and muskets of their own.

Clevercloggs had now made his way to the MC's platform. The little gnome grabbed up the microphone and shouted into it.

'Good people of Erthwurld, the RAE Rebellion has begun all over the Empire. It is time for each and every one of you to choose… are you for *Darkness*… or are you for *Light*?'

Responding to this, the home crowd rose up all over the Conquest Colosseum and shouted the Kernish rallying cry.

'Onen hag Oll!'

Tizzie now heard Mr Sand's familiar voice as he grabbed her left hand.

'We must go!'

She turned and was overjoyed to see he had hold of her brother with his right.

'LOUIS!'

'Hi, Tizzie.'

'This is not the time for all that,' said Mr Sand in an urgent tone. 'We must go… NOW!'

ONE HUNDRED & SIX

Rebellion On The Sea

Cule was on the HMS Kernow.

The ship was being pulled by whaleponies. This meant it had been able to cross the Citnalta Ocean in time for the start of the Gladiator Games at the Conquest Colosseum.

The whole RAE plan depended on a co-ordinated attack at the right time… the start of the Games.

Cule had been on deck training with the other Guardians of Kernow throughout much of the journey.

But now the real battle was about to commence.

They were heading for his homeland to take it back from the Evil Empire. The coastline of Land's End was already in sight.

As the whaleponies pulled the Kernish flagship towards shore, Cule looked North over the port side of the vessel.

He allowed himself a little smile of satisfaction as he saw the ships of the *RAE Force of Acirema North*.

Not long ago, he had witnessed an incredible sight: hundreds of eagleponies taking off from the decks of the ships, each carrying a rebel Redskin or Settler.

The young Kernish warrior hoped their mission to attack the Emperor's forces at the Conquest Colosseum would be successful.

He also hoped the rest of the mission of the RAE Force of Acirema North to take back the northern coast of Kernowland would result in victory.

Wondering how his girlfriend was getting on, Cule went over to the starboard side of the ship.

Looking down at the water, he saw Bella riding along on Dash at great speed.

He waved.

She waved back.

The young Sea Guardian was very happy that she had found Cule.

And she was also very happy that she could now see her beloved Kernowland on the horizon.

She, and the other dolphineers under her command, had been training on their dartingdolphins for much of the voyage from Acirema North.

Her squadron was determined to play its part in the mission to take back Falmouth Port and secure the south coast of Kernowland.

Bella had done all she could to make them ready for the coming battle.

ONE HUNDRED & SEVEN

Chaos In The Colosseum

The fighting in the Conquest Colosseum spilled over from the terraces and into the Arena of Blood.

There were soon thousands of people doing battle on the arena floor.

Seeing this, Evile hissed at Manaccan: 'Thiss iss whatt Ii gett forr lettingg amateurss arrangee thingss.' He then stood up, strode on to the platform, grabbed the microphone, and screamed dementedly into it.

'Soo youu wantt chaoss. Thenn Ii willl givee youu…

'CHAOSS!!!'

The Emperor waved his arms about dementedly, pointing in all directions as he issued instructions.

Somehow his orders got through to the keepers beneath the Colosseum floor. Acting quickly on their orders, the keepers released all the carnivorous beasts and Chewing Creatures through the trapdoors at the same time.

Chomp, Cyco, Grawl, and all the other beasts and creatures, rampaged about, trampling, mauling, and chewing as they went.

Just as Evile had promised, there was soon chaos in the Conquest Colosseum. There was roaring and screeching. There was yelling, and screaming, and running.

There were shots and explosions.

There was destruction and death.

ONE HUNDRED & EIGHT

RAE Rising: 'Onen Hag Oll!'

Elsewhere in Kernowland, members of RAE were taking back control of the castle. It was an inside job, and was certainly a more peaceful affair than the rebellion in the Colosseum.

Once again, Mrs Portwrinkle's pastys had been laced with a sleeping potion, and all the guards had been offered one. Naturally enough, every single one of them had eaten a piping hot pasty… and they were now peacefully sleeping at their posts.

Pemberley and Bude released all the loyal soldiers, including Sergeant Stout, who immediately ordered his men to put Evile's sleeping soldiers in the dungeons. The Kernish Flag was soon flying from the towers of Kernow Castle once more.

A similar thing was happening throughout Erthwurld.

The tribes and ordinary people were striking back against the Evil Empire, led by the members of RAE who had been planning this day for so long.

RAE was rising on every continent, taking back control of Erthwurld, so that Good and Right might be restored.

All the RAE Forces had adopted the Kernish rallying cry and they shouted it all over Erthwurld as they stood together in defiance of Evile and his Empire of Evil…

'Onen hag Oll!'
'One and All!'

ONE HUNDRED & NINE

Back To The Crystal Pool

Mr Sand pulled Tizzie and Louis along the Tunnel of Terror, down some steps, and into a deserted corridor.

After instructing the two children to line up, holding shoulders, behind him, he took out the Golden Key from his pocket and put the crystal end down on the hard stone floor.

'*Golden Cavern by the Power of Godolphin.*'

As soon as they had arrived back in the Golden Cavern, Mr Sand put his hand on the Crystal Door and said: 'Crystal Pool, Towan Blystra Beach, Kernowland, Eporue.'

The green crystal softened and the three of them linked arms and stepped into the door. Tizzie, Louis, and Mr Sand arrived back at the glistening cavern which contained the Crystal Pool.

'No need to go past the climbing crabs when you've got Crystal Doors and Golden Keys!' said Mr Sand with a smile.

'That's good,' said Louis, with a sigh of relief, as he remembered his encounter with the giant crabs on the beach.

'Now, you have both agreed to keep your adventures in Kernowland a secret,' said Mr Sand. 'So we don't want to arouse any unnecessary interest by you wearing these clothes from Erthwurld when you go back home.'

'But won't Mum and Dad know something's happened anyway?' asked Tizzie, as she and Louis removed their garments so that they were just wearing the swimming costumes they had arrived in. 'We've been gone for ages.'

'Well, that's where the magic of the Crystal Pool comes into play,' said Mr Sand.

'When you use the pool to travel between the dimensions, you can choose to arrive back at exactly the same time as you left, whichever way you go through.'

Louis was glad to hear this but was concerned for the well-being of Mr Sand and his other friends.

'What's going to happen in Kernowland and Erthwurld now, Mr Sand?'

'Well, the RAE Rebellion has begun and there is no turning back now.

'You saw the RAE Force of Acirema North attacking the Imperial Guard from their eagleponies at the Conquest Colosseum.

'We thought this would be the best time to begin the rebellion against the Emperor. And, just as we hoped, he had relaxed his defences because he'd just conquered the last kingdom on Erth that he didn't have in the Empire.

'As we speak, the rest of the RAE Force of Acirema North and the Guardians of Kernow should be landing on the northern and southern beaches of *Kernowland*... I will never call my country "Wonrekland"!

'All over Erthwurld, RAE Forces will be rising up and fighting the Empire, to take Erthwurld back for the good people.'

'But will you be okay, Mr Sand?'

'I honestly don't know, young man,' said the old solider. 'But sometimes we have to stand up and be counted in the fight for what is Good and Right, whatever the consequences. I *have* to play my part in the battle to try to defeat Evile. It is simply what I must do. But it was my first duty to do something else...

'...get you two home!

'In the Colosseum, since I'd finally got you both together in the same place at the same time, I had to use the opportunity to take you away from all this danger in our wurld and set you on your way home.

'It was a promise I made to King Kernow before he was killed by that nasty nephew of his.'

Mr Sand then looked at Louis as he said: 'Now, do you remember the password I gave you in the Dome Tower.'

'Yes, I remember,' said Louis.

'Good,' said Mr Sand.

'Thank you for helping us,' said Tizzie.

'It has been my pleasure,' said Mr Sand. 'In fact, it has been an honour to meet you both.'

Louis was fighting back a little tear of emotion as Mr Sand continued.

'Now remember, if you want to arrive home at exactly the same moment you left, you must say "same time" after the password.'

Louis nodded and managed a little smile for his kindly friend and teacher.

Mr Sand then watched as Tizzie and Louis stood on the sparkling blue rock and Louis said the password...

'I want to go to... CORNWALL... *same time*.'

ONE HUNDRED & TEN

Back To Echo Cave

Sssssssssssss.

The hard blue rock beneath their feet began to hiss.

The rock now went sticky, like glue, and their feet were stuck to it.

The rock got softer and softer until it was like runny jelly at the top but still quite firm under their feet.

It frothed and bubbled as blue steam rose all around them.

The children started to sink.

Tizzie and Louis looked at each other as they sank deeper and deeper into the steaming blue pool.

They weren't scared this time as they'd shared this experience before and knew just what to expect.

They were now up to their waists in the bubbling liquid.

As Louis' head was just about to go under, he gave one last smile to Mr Sand.

Mr Sand smiled warmly back as Louis sank below the surface of the steaming, frothing, bubbling blue liquid.

ONE HUNDRED & ELEVEN

Home At Last

The hard part of the rock under the Bennett children's feet began to rise up again.

Tizzie emerged from the bubbling, fizzing blue pool before Louis. First the top of her head, then her brow. When her eyes rose above the surface, she opened them and looked around. Just one more second to hold her breath.

'Ahhh,' she gasped, as her mouth was once more able to breathe air.

Then Louis' head emerged from the pool, followed by the rest of him. The pool began to solidify under their feet and soon, after a lot more hissing, they were standing on a firm slab of twinkling, sparkling blue rock again.

'Do you think we're back in Cornwall?' asked Louis.

'Well, Mr Sand has gone,' said Tizzie, 'so I should think so.'

'I hope he and the other good people win the battle against the Emperor and all those bad people,' said Louis.

'Of course they will,' reassured Tizzie. 'And then Erthwurld will be a nice place again.'

The children hurried down the windy tunnel.

A few moments later, they were back in Echo Cave.

Looking out, they could see people on the beach.

They saw two familiar faces from the cave entrance.

'MUM!'

'DAD!'

Tizzie and Louis ran across the beach, shouting and waving as great big tears of happiness streamed down their cheeks.

Mum and Dad both looked up at the same time.

They smiled and waved back as the two children ran even faster towards them.

Tizzie and Louis would never forget their adventures in Kernowland and Erthwurld.

But they were certainly glad to be home.

THE END

ERTH

GLACIERLAND

E

SNOWL

FJO

WILDLAND

E

ACIREMA NORTH

E

PRARIELAND

LAKELAND

Red Crystal

Tizzie

Ratlarbig Rock
Port of Acnalbasac
Isles of Airanac

Port Lujnab

CIFICAP OCEAN

QUAKELAND

SWAMPLAND

Abuc

CAVELAND

SA
Deser
Nv

CITNALTA OCEAN

AINAECO

E

E

RIVERLAND

Yellow Crystal

ACIREMA SOUTH

E

MOUNTAINLAND

Indigo Crystal

N

W   E

S

NREHTUOS OCEA

E

Or.